TOME OF MERCENARIES

CREDITS

GAME DESIGN: Robert Buckley

ADDITIONAL DESIGN: Keegan Geist (*Company of Bones, Caliban the Cruel, Leechtounges*), Robert N Moorhead (*The Most Illustrious Knights of the Order of* Drakonem Exterminatus*, Defenders of the Southern Reach & It's Lands And Bounties, Elite Griffon Knights*), Miguel F. Santiago Irizarry (*Farmers, Blood Ravens, Greenthumb Phalanx, Frontline Fanatics*), Juan Francisco Gonzalez Garza (*Mosscale Legion*), Paula Peterka (*The Devil's Nightmare Legion*)

DEVELOPER: Terran Empire Publishing

EDITORS: Terran Empire Publishing

MANAGING EDITOR: Robert Buckley

INTERIOR DESIGN AND LAYOUT: Robert Buckley

TERRAN EMPIRE PUBLISHING LOGO: Evan Rodda

COVER ARTIST: Evan Rodda

Who is Terran Empire Publishing?

Based in Northern California, USA, Terran Empire Publishing was founded in 2016 and specializes in fantasy and science fiction game products and books. With over 40 years of gaming experience, the team at Terran Empire Publishing promises to bring creative and unique takes on genre classics, as well as new material for gamers and readers of all ages.

Terran Empire Publishing
1761 Hillside Ct.
Placerville, CA 95667

Questions or Comments? Please email terranempire.comments@gmail.com!

 @terranempirepub

 Facebook.com/terranempirepublishing

 terranempirepublishing

TABLE OF CONTENTS

† Legendary Companies courtesy of Terran Empire Publishing's fans and Kickstarter backers

TERMS ARE STRUCK BETWEEN TWO MERCENARY COMPANIES

INTRODUCTION

A mercenary company is defined as a group of like minded individuals who participate in combat for the promise of rewards. Typically, companies form around a charismatic leader. A leader who not only displays prowess on the battlefield, but one who can also negotiate contracts and sustain the logistics needed to house, feed, and equip large groups of soldiers.

Other companies form from groups of soldiers who for what ever reason have no home to return to after a conflict is over. Often times, the army they belonged to was disbanded and they have no outlet in which to demonstrate their skill sets.

Whatever the reason for their formation, mercenary companies are needed in both times of war and peace. During conflicts, they can turn the tides of battle, augmenting the size of an attacking force and winning the day with expert tactics. During times of peace, mercenary companies are used to guard cities and towns, caravans, and wealthy manors or castles. They can be hired to deal with monsters, bandits, or worse. Most large cities have at least one mercenary company on retainer that they can quickly muster should the city be threatened.

There are two basic types of companies: *standing* and *recruited*. Standing companies are defined by always being together, and its members often do not have other occupations that would prevent them from leaving their regular life on short notice when a contract is signed.

Recruiting companies will often have a small, core group of veteran soldiers, including but not limited to its command structure. When a contract is taken, they recruit either from the local population, adventurers, or both. Sometimes they will put out a call for former members who have returned to their daily lives.

Some mercenary companies are a mixture of both basic types. They recruit as needed to fulfill a contract if their current roster is not sufficient to get the job done. Then, when the contract is fulfilled, the recruited soldiers return to their lives and can possibly be called on again should the need arise.

HOW TO USE THIS BOOK

The *Tome of Mercenaries* is a repository of groups that can be placed into adventures and campaigns as the GM sees fit. They can be used as antagonists the adventurers have to battle, fodder in a large war or conflict, or the adventurers themselves can join or form their own mercenary company.

Perhaps they have been contacted by a recruiter who is looking for a group of specialized troops for a specific contract. They can even be hired to infiltrate a corrupt mercenary company in order to disband them.

The following information describes how the entries in this book are laid out, and how to incorporate the data into your adventures and campaigns.

Name: This is the name of the mercenary company.

Nickname: These are the names the company is known as, either spoken by themselves or by others.

Symbol: This is the symbol the company displays on their equipment and flags.

Type: This entry will describe the kind of company; *Standing* (together at all times), *Recruiting* (recruits as needed), *Fixed* (has a permanent headquarters), *Roaming* (has no permanent headquarters or has several bases of operations)

Size: This is the size of the company's permanent members. If a number is displayed in brackets, this is the usual number the company recruits to fulfill contracts. A second number is given to represent the number of camp followers that travel with the company when fulfilling large contracts.

Cost: The first number is the amount expected when the contract is signed. The second number is the amount needed per day. The third number is the amount estimated for additional expenses that may arise while fulfilling the contract.

Leader: This describes the leader of the mercenary company.

Captains: Generally, a mercenary company will have at least one captain who acts as the leader when he or she is otherwise indisposed. Some companies have several captains who are in charge of individual units. If a company has more than one captain, the head captain and the one who is second in command is identified with a * by their entry.

Lieutenants: A mercenary company is nothing without its chain-of-command structure. The lieutenants get orders from the captains or from the company's leader directly, and in turn, pass those instructions to the soldiers while making sure they are followed correctly.

Alignment: This is the average alignment of the mercenary company. Individual alignments can vary.

Formation: This entry describes the units within the mercenary company. Soldier types in *italics* represent the average soldier and are described in the NPC chapter or at the end of the company's listing.

Expertise: This section describes the mercenary company's area of expertise and the types of contracts they usually take on. **Guard Duty** consists of guarding goods and property. **Single/Sustained Battle** consists of participating in a single decisive battle or a series of smaller battles in rapid succession. **War** consists of sustained campaigns that can include sieges or the storming of fortified positions.

Trustworthiness: This is a numerical value placed on the overall reliability of the mercenary company ranging from 1 to 5, with 1 being *low/dishonest* and 5 being *high/honest*. An honest company will follow a contract through to its completion. A dishonest company will weigh consequences of breaking a contract and likely do what is best for themselves.

Base: The mercenary company's base of operations is discussed here.

Sphere of Operations: This will discuss where the company is likely to be found and where it is currently operating. Locations are based in the #world of Shin'ar, but they can easily be molded into any campaign setting.

Government: This entry will describe how the company makes its decisions. See the associated **sidebar** for more information.

Tactics: This entry will go on to describe the general tactics used by the mercenary company on and off the battlefield.

Logistics: This will describe the general arms and equipment used by the company.

History: This entry describes the founding of the company, its most notable contracts, and other information regarding the company and its members.

Notable NPCs: Most often, this entry will give statistics for soldier types that are unique to the mercenary company.

SIZE	NUMBER OF MEMBERS
Squad	10 to 25
Troop	26 to 60
Battalion	61 to 120
Brigade	121 - 250
Regiment	251 - 400
Legion	401+

MERCENARY COMPANY SIZE

GOVERNMENT TYPES

Military. The company has a strict chain-of-command, based on familiar military hierarchies.

Council. The company is run by a council of veterans or founding members.

Dictatorship. The company is run by a single individual.

Democratic. The company issues a vote on relevant policies and contracts. Typically, each solider gets a single vote, and a majority is needed to win. A single leader is chosen by votes and leads for a predetermined amount of time.

Brotherhood. Similar to a democratic government, members get a single vote, though it is not uncommon for the leadership to dictate a course of action instead. Each member is also a sworn brother to the next, and that oath is what keeps them together.

Clan. The company is, in essence, a group of familiarly linked individuals who all belong to the same demographic group.

Often times, a mercenary company will be a mixture of two or more government types, such as a Military Dictatorship or a Democratic Council.

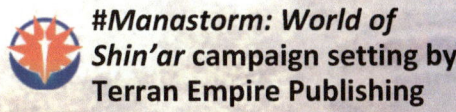
#Manastorm: World of Shin'ar campaign setting by Terran Empire Publishing

CHAPTER ONE
MAJOR PLAYERS

Name: The Bronze Scales

Nickname: Scale Brotherhood, Dullscales

Symbol: A stylized bronze dragon on an argent and black field. Flown on flags but never worn on armor or clothing.

Type: Recruiting/Roaming

Size: Legion; 100 (530)/100

Cost: 2200 gp/200 gp/280 gp per week

Leader: Acri the Bronze (Ancient Bronze Dragon)

Captains: 3; *Zoilous Skelor (N Zevrish male Fighter 17), Ilgiz Khamtova (CN Human male Cleric 14), Alvir *von* Kramperdon (LN Calvoid male Wizard 16)

Lieutenants: 6

Alignment: N

Formation: The Bronze Scales typically form up 350 *light foot* and 100 *heavy foot* as their main combat force. They are supported by 100 *mercenary archers*, 10 *mercenary acolytes*, and 5 *mercenary priests*. A force of 25 *centaur lancers* is held back until the infantry makes an opening. If an opening does not present itself, 25 *Zevrish skirmishers* are deployed to force one open. Rounding out the company are 15 *mercenary wizards* who are sprinkled into the various units, depending on the magical might the opposing force brings to bear.

Expertise: Guard Duty, Single/Sustained Battle, War

Trustworthiness: 5

Base: Bronzeville; Empire of Alteria (Zava Hills), Tower of Bronze; Kala Dominion (Eastern Province), Fort Dullscale; Eastern Cliffs

Sphere of Operations: Empire of Alteria (mainland), Kala Dominion (Eastern Province), Kingdom of Jutan (Clawbite Hills), Starfall Sea (Mumbay)

Government: Dictatorship

Tactics: The Bronze Scales deploy tight formations and, discipline within the ranks is high. Soldiers quickly find out that disappointing an ancient dragon is a position they do not want to find themselves in.

The infantry is the backbone of the company, and the Bronze Scales are distinguished on the battlefield by their bronze-colored armor and shields. A favored tactic is to soften the opposing force with arrows while the Zevrish skirmishers probe and attack weak points. When an opening is made, the centaur lancers charge in, further widening the hole and allowing the infantry to pour in.

When the company accepts a contract, the signing bonus is transferred right into Acri's personal hoard, minus a few hundred coins for his captains. They do not accept contracts that force them to fight Alterian Legion troops or contracts that go against the best interest of the Alterian Senate. Acri is careful to keep himself in good standing within the Empire.

Logistics: Soldiers are equipped with **above average** arms and equipment. Every soldier is given a *potion of healing* before a battle, as well as *potions of climbing* or similar magic, depending on the terrain and objective of the fight. Lieutenants are given magical versions of the weapons and armor that their unit uses. There is a 30% chance an individual soldier will have a magic weapon or common/uncommon item, as well.

History: When Acri first came to Shin'ar, he worked out an agreement with the Alterian Senate to allow him to build a lair within their borders. Within ten years, Bronzeville grew from a simple cave complex dug into the western Zava Hills, to a noisy hamlet full of practicing soldiers and adventuring bands. Acri controls Bronzeville and allows those who please him to use the place to rest, train and re-equip themselves before heading back out into the world.

Not content on forming and equipping adventuring bands for a share of their profits, Acri tasked his aide and friend Zoilous Skelor to build a mercenary force that would take contracts around the world. The Bronze Scales first saw victory battling rouge Aravork forces in the Eastern Cliffs. The airborne raiders were dealt a mighty blow by the company that allowed merchants to travel along the grasslands in relative peace. True to his Draconic lust for coin, Acri promptly withdrew his forces once the contract to stabilize the region was done, and did not deploy them again until a new contract was signed and the funds transferred to his hoard.

When the Kala Dominion reopened their borders to foreign travelers, the Lord High General contracted the Bronze Scales to help police Shadow Gap, the only area the Dominion allowed foreigners to enter their territory.

The company maintains a small tower near the Shadow Gap to help facilitate this ongoing contract.

Acri is well liked in the Empire of Alteria, and especially by the ruling Atlanteans. He is often seen in Atlantis and Sprata, dining with prominent officials and meeting with representatives of the Alterian Senate.

Notable NPCs. Centaur Lancer, Zevrish Skirmisher

CENTAUR LANCER

Large Monstrosity, N

ARMOR CLASS
20 (plate mail, shield)
HIT POINTS
45 (6d10+12)
SPEED
40 ft.

STR 18 (+4) DEX 14 (+2) CON 14 (+2) INT 10 (+0) WIS 13 (+1) CHA 11 (+0)

SKILLS Athletics +6, Perception +3, Survival +3
SENSES passive Perception 13
LANGUAGES Sylvan, Alterian
CHALLENGE 3 (700 xp)

Charge. If the centaur lancer moves at least 30 feet straight toward a target then hits it with a lance attack on the same turn, the target takes an extra 10 (3d6) piercing damage.

Martial Advantage. Once per turn, the centaur lancer can deal an extra 7 (2d6) damage to a creature it hits with a weapon attack if that creature is within 5 feet of an ally of the centaur lancer that isn't incapacitated.

ACTIONS

Multiattack. The centaur lancer makes two melee attacks.

Lance. Melee Weapon Attack: +6 to hit, reach 10 ft.; One target. Hit: 10 (1d12+4) piercing damage.

Hooves. Melee Weapon Attack: +6 to hit, reach 5 ft.; One target. Hit: 11 (2d6+4) bludgeoning damage.

Shortsword. Melee Weapon Attack: +6 to hit, reach 5 ft.; One target. Hit: 8 (1d6+4) piercing damage.

EQUIPMENT

Plate mail, shield, lance, shortsword, mercenary pack

ZEVRISH SKIRMISHER

Medium Humanoid (Zevrish), Any alignment

ARMOR CLASS
17 (breastplate, shield)
HIT POINTS
25 (4d8+8)
SPEED
20 ft.

STR 16 (+3) DEX 12 (+1) CON 15 (+2) INT 10 (+0) WIS 11 (+0) CHA 12 (+1)

SKILLS Athletics +5, Intimidation +3, Stealth +3
SENSES passive Perception 10
LANGUAGES Zava, Alterian
CHALLENGE 2 (450 xp)

Improved Critical. The Zevrish skirmisher makes a critical strike on a roll of 19 or 20.

Sneak Attack. Once per turn, the Zevrish skirmisher deals an extra 7 (2d6) damage when it hits a target with a weapon attack and has *advantage* on the attack roll, or when the target is within 5 feet of an ally of the Zevrish skirmisher that isn't *incapacitated* and the Zevrish skirmisher does not have *disadvantage* on the attack roll.

ACTIONS

Battleaxe. Melee Weapon Attack: +5 to hit, reach 5 ft.; One target. Hit: 8 (1d8+3) slashing damage or 9 (1d10+3) slashing damage if wielded with two hands.

Shortsword. Melee Weapon Attack: +5 to hit, reach 5 ft.; One target. Hit: 7 (1d6+3) piercing damage.

Javelin. Melee or Ranged Weapon Attack: +5 to hit, range 5 feet, or 30/120 feet. One target. Hit: 7 (1d6+3) piercing damage.

EQUIPMENT

Breastplate, shield, battleaxe, shortsword, 5 javelins, mercenary pack

Name: The Brotherhood of the Shining Shield

Nickname: Bright-shields, Shining Knights, The Shining Shields

Symbol: A golden trinity knot on an argent field. Flown on flags and displayed on shields.

Type: Standing/Fixed

Size: Brigade; 205/30

Cost: 1800 gp/300 gp/100 gp per week

Leader: Inigo Piacenza de Fatera (LG Human male Paladin 16)

Captains: 4; *Diogo Stuza de Fatera (LG Human male Paladin 14), Ana Soares de Broncho (LG Human female Cleric 14), Dorvin *vos* Hippernel (LN Calvoid male Wizard 6/Cleric 6)

Lieutenants: 4

Alignment: LG

Formation: The Shining Shields form up 80 *light foot* and 20 *heavy foot* as their main attacking force. A unit comprising of 15 *heavy mounted* and 15 *mounted paladins* serve as the company's calvary, and they are further assisted by 20 *mercenary archers*, 25 *mercenary acolytes*, and 15 *mercenary priests*. A small unit of 15 *mercenary wizards* moves about the battlefield supporting where they are needed most.

Expertise: Guard Duty, Single/Sustained Battle

Trustworthiness: 5

Base: Shield Brother Keep; City-State of Fatera (Verigal)

Sphere of Operations: Verigal (Sylvar, Palous), Eastern Cliffs, Empire of Alteria (Zava Hills)

Government: Brotherhood

Tactics: The Shining Shields form tight ranks born of constant drills and severe punishments for repeat offenders. They have never been known to flee combat, especially when bolstered by the words and deeds of their pious brothers.

When accepting a new contract, half of the signing bonus goes straight to the Temple of Aquaris in the City-State of Fatera, which in turn uses the funds to distribute food and clean water to the poor of that city. The Shining Shields are well-loved in that city and in the towns and villages surrounding it. Inigo and his captains have been known to "loan out" soldiers to some of those villages as guards against monsters and bandits.

Payment for such services is expected in room and boarding for the soldiers and donations to local temples of Aquaris.

Logistics: The Shining Shields have **above average** arms and equipment. New soldiers are given a *shield +1* embossed with the company's symbol when they join the Brotherhood. Simple *potions of healing* and similar magic are handed out before large battles. Lieutenants all have either a magical weapon or suit of armor, and 15% of individual soldiers will have a personal common or uncommon magic item or weapon.

History: The Brotherhood of the Shining Shields formed ten years ago when the then novice paladin Inigo Piacenza returned from an expedition to the East. He saw the rampant corruption that has taken hold of most of the mercenary companies that ply their trade in the eastern city-states and vowed to create a company that could be relied upon to always do the right thing. With the help of his good friend Diogo and the church of Aquaris in Fatera, the Shining Shields was born.

The church officially has nothing to do with the operation of the mercenary company, though they do readily accept donations from Inigo, and their clerics regularly sign on for tours of duty with the company. The Shining Shields will never take a contract that would have them directly or indirectly harm innocents.

Recently, the company was hired to protect merchant traffic along the roads from Fatera to the City-State of Chaven. It is believed that brigands in the employ of the City-State of Medra have begun to waylay caravans in hopes to destabilize trade in the region.

A Paladin of the Shining Shields escorts a young woman along a forested trail.

Name: Crimson Draconia
Nickname: Red Dragons, Crimson Fire
Symbol: A snarling red dragon face on a black background. Flown on flags and displayed on shields.
Type: Standing/Fixed
Size: Regiment; 260/80
Cost: 2800 gp/280 gp/500 gp per week
Leader: Alturian Bloodeye (LE Red Dragonborn male Fighter 8/Rogue 5)
Captains: 2; *Urian Draco (LE Red Dragonborn male Sorcerer 13), Gelinda of the Red Mist (CE Red Dragonborn female Barbarian 9)
Lieutenants: 4
Alignment: LE
Formation: Crimson Draconia's main attacking force is made up of 125 *heavy foot*. They are supported by 80 *mercenary archers*, 18 *mercenary acolytes*, 2 *mercenary priests*, and 30 *mercenary sorcerers*. Their most feared troops are the 5 *dragon riders* deployed ahead of the main force to disrupt enemy lines with fire from above.
Expertise: Single/Sustained Battle, War
Trustworthiness: 4
Base: Castle Draconia; Firepeaks
Sphere of Operations: Damp Forest, Kala Dominion (Western Province), Kingdom of Jutan (Clawbite Hills), Empire of Alteria (Northern Hinterlands)
Government: Clan
Tactics: The dragon riders are typically sent out first. Often times, just the sight of five red dragons bearing down on them is enough to get the enemy's front ranks fleeing. Once a route is in effect, the main force closes in, backed by the archers and sorcerers.

Alturian has enlisted the aid of a clutch of red dragons that lair in the Firepeaks. In exchange for large sums of gold, five young red dragons have signed on with the company for a period of 10 years. A third of the signing bonus and all of the per week expenses go to the dragons. They currently have four years left, and most signs point to them re-enlisting as the gold they have collected for their services have made them very rich, even by a dragon's standards.

Logistics: Crimson Draconia's soldiers employ **above average** arms and armor. The company is distinct in its dress. Armor is dyed black and red, and often times embellished spikes are crafted into the armor and shields worn by the company's heavy foot

soldiers. Magical items are sparse among the average soldier; however, captains and lieutenants each have numerous personal magical items and weapons.

History: During a turbulent time in the planet's history known as a Lunar Quickening, a large clan of Red Dragonborn emerged from a portal that opened high up in the Firepeak Mountains. Days later, the portal abruptly closed, stranding the clan on the planet. Fortunately for them, the place in which they chose to settle was a range of mountains that included several inactive volcanoes. The clan thrived in this environment and quickly came to dominate the area.

As the clan grew in size, its members began to explore the new world. They found many different races living in close proximity to each other. The races, for the most part, were emigrants as well to this planet, and the mixing of so many cultures inevitably caused arguments and conflict. Seeing the need for trained soldiers, the clan began to form up and sell their services to whoever came calling.

Notable NPCs: Dragon Rider, Young Red Dragon

DRAGON RIDER

Medium Humanoid (Red Dragonborn), LE

ARMOR CLASS
16 (scale mail, shield)
HIT POINTS
50 (5d10+12)
SPEED
30 ft.

| STR 18 (+4) | DEX 11 (+0) | CON 17 (+3) | INT 11 (+0) | WIS 12 (+1) | CHA 11 (+0) |

SKILLS Animal Handling +2, Perception +3
DAMAGE RESISTANCE Fire
SENSES passive Perception 11
LANGUAGES Draconic, Tradespeech
CHALLENGE 2 (450 xp)

Archery. The dragon rider gains a +2 bonus to ranged attack rolls.

Action Surge. The dragon rider can take one additional action on top of their regular action and a possible bonus action. They can do this once before a short rest.

ACTIONS

Breath Weapon. The dragon rider can exhale a 15-foot cone of fire, dealing 7 (2d6) fire damage to any creature in the radius that fails a DC 13 Dexterity saving throw. The breath weapon recharges after a short or long rest.

Flail. *Melee Weapon Attack*: +6 to hit, reach 5 ft.; One target. Hit: 9 (1d8+4) bludgeoning damage.

Javelin. *Melee or Ranged Weapon Attack*: +6 or +8 to hit, reach 5 feet or 20/60 feet; One target. Hit: 8 (1d6+4) piercing damage.

EQUIPMENT

Scale mail, shield, flail, 8 javelins, mercenary pack, sac of dried meat (dragon snacks), military saddle

ACTIONS

Multiattack. The dragon makes three attacks: one with its bite and two with its claws.

Bite. *Melee Weapon Attack*: +10 to hit, reach 10 ft.; One target. Hit: 17 (2d10+6) piercing damage plus 3 (1d6) fire damage.

Claw. *Melee Weapon Attack*: +10 to hit, reach 5 ft.; One target. Hit: 13 (2d6+6) slashing damage.

Fire Breath (Recharge 5-6). The dragon exhales fire in a 30-foot cone. Each creature in that area must make a DC 17 Dexterity saving throw, taking 56 (16d6) fire damage on a failed save, or half as much damage on a successful one.

YOUNG RED DRAGON

Large Dragon, CE

ARMOR CLASS
18 (natural armor)

HIT POINTS
178 (17d10+85)

SPEED
40 ft.; Climb 40 ft.; Fly 80 ft.

STR 23 (+6) DEX 10 (+0) CON 21 (+5) INT 14 (+2) WIS 11 (+0) CHA 19 (+4)

SAVING THROWS Dexterity +4, Constitution +9, Wisdom +4, Charisma +8

SKILLS Perception +8, Stealth +4

DAMAGE IMMUNITY
Fire

SENSES Blindsight 30 ft.; Darkvision 120 ft.; passive Perception 18

LANGUAGES Draconic

CHALLENGE 10 (5,900 xp)

Name: The Darkblades of Jutan

Nickname: Darkblades, Black Blades

Symbol: Three black swords intertwined facing down. The symbol is displayed on shields, banners, and over the breast on surcoats and armor.

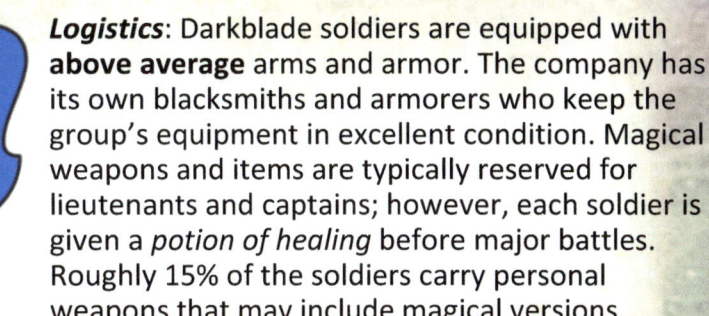

Type: Standing/Fixed

Size: Brigade; 175/80

Cost: 1200 gp/250 gp/100 gp per week

Leader: Ser Rallo Ulfinson (LN Human male Fighter 14)

Captains: 4; *Ser Afli Vistok (LN Human male †Anointed Knight 11 of Marvela), Ridder Borghild Lofgren (LN Human female Anointed Knight 9), Thorvid Olegson (LG Human male Cleric 11), Klyppr Hjorth (LN Human male Wizard 10)

Lieutenants: 8

Alignment: LN

Formation: The Darkblades consist of 40 *light foot* and 40 *heavy foot* that make up the front line soldiers. A force of 30 *heavy mounted* is held as a reserve cavalry. They have 15 *mercenary archers* and 5 *mercenary ambushers* who they deploy ahead of the main force to scout and harass enemy positions. A group of 5 *mercenary acolytes* and 5 *mercenary priests* accompany the main force in battle A recent addition to the company is a group of 15 *mercenary berserkers* who act as front line skirmishers. The company has a small contingent of magic users, numbering only 10 *mercenary wizards* who are sprinkled into the various units as they are needed.

Expertise: Guard Duty, Single/Sustained Battle

Trustworthiness: 5

Base: Darkblade Keep; Jarland of the Crownlands (Kingdom of Jutan)

Sphere of Operations: The Kingdom of Jutan (Crownlands, The Basket, Southern Shore, Clawbite Hills), The Jutal Forest, Lake of Ice

Government: Military Council

Tactics: The Darkblades employ typical tactics when engaged in large scale battles. Their formations are tight, and discipline is strict. Soldiers assigned to guard duty do so with respect and attention to detail that one can expect from a well-disciplined group of mercenaries. They are known for completing contracts quickly and with practiced efficiency.

Logistics: Darkblade soldiers are equipped with **above average** arms and armor. The company has its own blacksmiths and armorers who keep the group's equipment in excellent condition. Magical weapons and items are typically reserved for lieutenants and captains; however, each soldier is given a *potion of healing* before major battles. Roughly 15% of the soldiers carry personal weapons that may include magical versions.

History: Founded eighteen years ago by Rallo Ulfinson and his good friend, Afli Vistok, the Darkblades were formed from the remnants of a force conscripted by the government of Jutan to deal with the rise of banditry in the outlying counties of the Jarland of the Crownlands. The army, which was made up of both professional soldiers and conscripted men, managed to uncover a network of allied bandit groups that were plaguing the small communities and homesteads.

After breaking the bandits hold on the region, most of the conscripted soldiers went back to their lives. Enough, however, remained that shared the same goal as Rallo and Afli; to form a mercenary group that always fought on the right side of the law. Early contracts were completed quickly and always with a satisfying outcome, rapidly increasing the company's reputation as a group of skilled and trustworthy soldiers.

As the company grew, they began to take contracts outside of the Crownlands and the Kingdom of Jutan all together. Units of Darkblades can be found guarding logging camps in the Jutal Forest, rooting out goblins and trolls in the Clawbite Hills, and battling albino lizardmen around the Lake of Ice.

It was around the Lake of Ice that the company first ran afoul of the Snow Vipers, a small group of killers who sell their talents to the highest bidder. The two groups found themselves on the opposite sides of a conflict between neighboring settlements. During the night, the Snow Vipers infiltrated the Darkblade camp and slew over a dozen men, including a captain and two lieutenants, before being discovered and chased off. In retaliation, the Darkblades used what magical might they could muster to conjure a large fireball that fully consumed the Snow Viper camp, killing a large number of troops and severely wounding their leader.

†Anointed Knight described in *Manastorm: World of Shin'ar*

The Darkblades are known for turning away individuals who try to join the company who display overly aggressive and intolerable behavior. They pride themselves on their excellent reputation, a reputation that keeps them in the royal family's good graces and keeps a steady stream of coin flowing from noble houses and wealthy merchants alike.

Name: Order of the Boar's Head

Nickname: Tuskers, Boarsmen

Symbol: A black boar's head, facing sinister. Often depicted on a white background and flown on flags. Various units use a variation of the symbol in their unit flags and displayed colors.

Type: Standing/Roaming

Size: Legion; 470/160

Cost: 2000 gp/325 gp/140 per week

Leader: General Comita Basalero (N Zevrish female Fighter 16)

Captains: 3; *Charl Terzieff (N Half-Atlantean/Human male Wizard 16), Apollos Gilabas (CN Zevrish male Cleric 11), Bjorjor Ralfson (N Human male Bard 9)

Lieutenants: 10

Alignment: N

Formation: The Order of the Boar's Head fields 170 *light foot* accompanied by 80 *heavy foot* on the battlefield. Deployed among them are 35 *mercenary acolytes* and 15 *mercenary priests*. A force of 60 *mercenary archers* and 50 *heavy mounted* are held behind the main attacking force. A unit of 25 *horselord skirmishers* is deployed with the main army, while a group of 25 *ogre shock troopers* acts as the company's vanguard.

Expertise: Guard Duty, Single/Sustained Battle, War

Trustworthiness: 5

Base: Castle Epak'nopt; Empire of Alteria (Northern Hinterlands), Fort Thunder; Damp Forest, Karzik Keep; Empire of Alteria (Estanyan Plains)

Sphere of Operations: Empire of Alteria (mainland), Kingdom of Jutan (Clawbite Hills); Damp Forest; Verigal (Sylvar)

Government: Military Dictatorship

Tactics: The Order of the Boar's Head is an impressive sight to see. The noise of perfectly ordered foot-soldiers marching in step is deafening. Add in the thunderous sound from the horselord skirmishers as they race up and down the battlefield, screaming and firing arrows from horseback with perfect precision, and you have a real cacophony of war.

Their leader, General Comita Basalero, is as much feared as loved by her troops. She is known to shower affection and praise upon units that show tenacity, intellect, and courage on the battlefield. She is also known to personally whip soldiers who flee or refuse a direct order. The Order takes any contract, and they do not worry about which side is right or which side is wrong. As long as the coin is paid, the Boarsmen will fight.

Logistics: The Order of the Boar's Head equips its troops with **above average** arms and armor. Captains and lieutenants all have magical versions of the typical gear assigned to soldiers in their care. *Potions of healing* are handed out before conflicts, and additional potions can be purchased, at a discount, from the Order's quartermaster. Almost 30% of the company's soldiers will have a personal common or uncommon magical item or weapon.

History: Two dozen years ago, an old soldier named Herondus Basalero returned home from his eighth tour of duty with the Alterian Legion to find his family homeless and destitute. While he was away, his wife made a series of bad investments, one after another, and the coin he sent back home quickly evaporated. Unable to soldier anymore due to numerous injuries sustained in the service of his empire, Herondus began to train his children in the art of war in hopes they would eventually join the Legions as elite soldiers, thus earning a higher salary.

When his eldest child came of age, she attempted to join the Legion but was turned away. Unaware to Herondus, a rival soldier from his days in the Legion had obtained an officer's rank. It was he who dismissed Herondus' daughter and blacklisted any of his children from service. Dismayed, but not beaten, Herondus began to frequent taverns and feasthalls looking for ex-soldiers who were in a similar situation. Six months later, the Order of the Boar's Head was established, with a crippled Herondus leading a force of 35 aging legionnaires.

The first year saw the meager group hired for simple caravan guard duty and manual labor. The work was hard on the old-timers, but the coin was steady, and they soon became known for their prowess and acumen in battle. They began to hire more soldiers and take larger contracts.

Herondus would pass away two years after the formation of the mercenary company, and leadership passed to his eldest child, Comita. It was her intellect and head for finances that saw the company's star soar, as they began to take contracts directly from the Alterian Senate. That revenue stream allowed them to hire and train more soldiers, and construct their base in the Alterian Hinterlands.

The Order of the Boar's Head is entirely professional when taking contracts. Promises made are promises kept by General Comita, and her soldiers have distinguished themselves on hundreds of battlefields.

Notable NPCs: Horselord Skirmisher, Ogre Shock Trooper

HORSELORD SKIRMISHER

Medium Humanoid (Human), CN

ARMOR CLASS
16 (scale mail)
HIT POINTS
35 (4d10+8)
SPEED
30 ft.

STR 15 (+2) DEX 15 (+2) CON 14 (+2) INT 10 (+0) WIS 12 (+1) CHA 14 (+2)

SKILLS Animal Handling +4, Acrobatics +4, Stealth +4
SENSES passive Perception 11
LANGUAGES Estan, Alterian
CHALLENGE 2 (450 xp)

Horselord Charge. If the horselord skirmisher moves at least 30 feet straight toward a target then hits it with a melee weapon attack on the same turn, the target takes an extra 7 (2d6) damage.

Mounted Archery. The horselord skirmisher gains a +2 bonus to ranged attack rolls while riding a mount.

ACTIONS

Multiattack. The horselord skirmisher makes two shortbow attacks or two scimitar attacks.

Shortbow. *Ranged Weapon Attack:* +6 to hit, range 80/320 ft.; One target. Hit: 6 (1d6+2) piercing damage.

Scimitar. *Melee Weapon Attack:* +4 to hit, reach 5 ft.; One target. Hit: 6 (1d6+2) slashing damage.

EQUIPMENT

Scale mail, shortbow, quiver with 20 arrows, scimitar, mercenary pack, trained riding horse, military saddle

OGRE SHOCK TROOPER

Large Giant, LE

ARMOR CLASS
17 (splint mail, shield)
HIT POINTS
59 (7d10+21)
SPEED
40 ft.

STR 19 (+4) DEX 08 (-1) CON 16 (+3) INT 08 (-1) WIS 08 (-1) CHA 08 (-1)

SENSES Darkvision 60 ft.; passive Perception 09
LANGUAGES Giant, Alterian
CHALLENGE 3 (700 xp)

Aggressive. As a bonus action, the ogre shock trooper can move up to its speed toward a hostile creature that it can see.

ACTIONS

Warhammer. *Melee Weapon Attack:* +6 to hit, reach 5 ft.; One target. Hit: 9 (1d8+4) bludgeoning damage.

EQUIPMENT

Splint mail, shield, warhammer, mercenary pack, sac of shiny trinkets

Name: Order of the Keg

Nickname: Brown Barrels

Symbol: A barrel or keg on a white field. Displayed primarily on shields and flags. Some units show the symbol on badges or on surcoats.

Type: Standing/Fixed

Size: Regiment; 290/50

Cost: 800 gp/260 gp/100 gp per week

Leader: Omorian Roundkeg (LN Dwarf male Fighter 19)

Captains: 5; *Riswynn Roundkeg (LN Dwarf female Fighter 12), Dain Roundkeg (LN Dwarf male Cleric 14), Thorin Roundkeg (LN Dwarf male Wizard 9), Torgga Splinterkeg (CN Dwarf female Barbarian 11), Oskar O' the Stones (LN Dwarf male Fighter 6/Ranger 5)

Lieutenants: 6

Alignment: LN

Formation: The Order of the Keg fields an impressive 135 stout dwarven *heavy foot* on the battlefield, accompanied by 60 *dwarven crossbowmen*. A small force of 20 *mercenary acolytes* and 15 *mercenary priests* are sprinkled into the front line units, while a roaming band of 8 *mercenary wizards* supports the ranks from the rear. A unit of 30 *mercenary berserkers* acts as skirmishers, and the company fields 22 *siege weapon operators* behind the lines who man and fire mobile ballista and catapults.

Expertise: Guard Duty, Single/Sustained Battle, War

Trustworthiness: 4

Base: The Keg (castle); City-State of Montero (Verigal)

Sphere of Operations: Verigal (Palous, Sylvar, North Sea), Dark Sun Woods, Eltra

Government: Clan Council

Tactics: Rowdy but disciplined, the dwarves known as the Brown Barrels march onto a battlefield in perfect step, loudly singing a dwarven fight song. One of their most impressive tactics is known as the Angry Turtle. The foot soldiers lock shields in a full-cover maneuver that allows the crossbowmen to pick and choose targets while remaining safe behind the shield-wall.

As the "Turtle" inches forward, the unit of foam-at-the-mouth berserkers explodes from cover laying waste to any type of force sent to disrupt the shield-wall.

The Order of the Keg takes contracts that allow them to display their prowess and keep them swimming in ale for the foreseeable future.

Logistics: The company's soldiers are equipped with **superb** arms and armor. Breaks, tears, and blunt weapons are fixed daily, allowing the soldiers to meet the enemy with perfectly maintained equipment and weapons, every time. Though the company lacks any type of sizable magical force, its captains and lieutenants all sport magical weapons and armor. Simple potions, such as *potions of healing*, are readily available upon request. An estimated 15% of the company's soldiers will have a personal common or uncommon magical item.

History: The planet of Shin'ar is known for its turbulent magical storms known as Manastorms. During one such storm, a random portal to an underground city opened up. Though no larger than an ogre, the portal remained open for weeks, allowing the inhabitants of that underground city to explore the cold mountain valley that was magically opened to them. While the portal was open, three clans of Dwarves first sent scouts, and then after meeting and coming to an agreement with the humans who lived in the valley, they began to send colonists.

They were warned that the portal would not remain open forever, and the dwarves would most likely be marooned on the planet. This news sent many of the colonists back home; however, about 200 of adventurous dwarves remained when the portal finally closed. The majority of the newcomers hailed from the Roundkeg Clan, a clan that was infamous for its parties and drunken brawling.

After establishing a living space for the clan, many of the elders saw the conflict rich environment that was Verigal as the perfect place to earn some coin while demonstrating their advanced dwarven fighting techniques. The Order of the Keg was a welcome addition to the ranks of mercenary companies that ply their trade for the City-States.

Notable NPCs. Dwarven Crossbowmen, Siege Weapon Operator

DWARVEN CROSSBOWMEN

Medium Humanoid (Dwarf), Any alignment

ARMOR CLASS
15 (scale mail)
HIT POINTS
30 (3d10+9)
SPEED
30 ft.

STR 17 (+3) DEX 13 (+1) CON 17 (+3) INT 10 (+0) WIS 11 (+0) CHA 10 (+0)

SKILLS Athletics +5, Survival +2
SENSES Darkvision 60 ft.; passive Perception 10
LANGUAGES Dwarvish, Tradespeech
CHALLENGE 1 (200 xp)

Archery. The dwarven crossbowmen gains a +2 bonus to attack rolls with ranged weapons.

ACTIONS

Heavy Crossbow. Ranged Weapon Attack: +5 to hit, range 100/400 ft.; One target. Hit: 7 (1d10+1) piercing damage.
Shortsword. Melee Weapon Attack: +5 to hit, reach 5 ft.; One target. Hit: 7 (1d6+3) piercing damage.

EQUIPMENT

Scale mail, heavy crossbow, crossbow bolt case with 40 crossbow bolts, shortsword, mercenary pack, personal tankard

Ballista (Large Object)

AC 15; **HP** 50; **Damage Immunities**: poison, psychic

A ballista is a massive crossbow that fires heavy bolts. Before it can be fired it must be loaded and aimed. It takes one action to load the weapon, one action to aim, and one action to fire it.

SIEGE WEAPON OPERATOR

Medium Humanoid (Dwarf), Any alignment

ARMOR CLASS
14 (ring mail)
HIT POINTS
30 (3d10+9)
SPEED
30 ft.

STR 17 (+3) DEX 10 (+0) CON 17 (+3) INT 12 (+1) WIS 12 (+1) CHA 10 (+0)

SKILLS Athletics +5, Perception +3
SENSES Darkvision 60 ft.; passive Perception 13
LANGUAGES Dwarvish, Tradespeech
CHALLENGE 1 (200 xp)

Zeroed In. The siege weapon operator gains a +2 bonus to ranged weapon attacks while firing a siege weapon.

ACTIONS

Shortsword. Melee Weapon Attack: +5 to hit, reach 5 ft.; One target. Hit: 7 (1d6+3) piercing damage.
Bolt. Ranged Weapon Attack: +4 to hit, range 120/480 ft.; One target. Hit: 16 (3d10) piercing damage.
Catapult Stone. Ranged Weapon Attack: +4 to hit, range 300/1,200 ft. (Can't hit targets within 60 feet of it); One target. Hit: 44 (8d10) bludgeoning damage.

EQUIPMENT

Ring mail, shortsword, mercenary pack, personal tankard

Catapult (Huge Object)
AC 15; **HP** 150; **Damage Immunities**: poison, psychic

A catapult is a powerful siege engine that can hurl its payload in a high arc, so it can hit targets behind cover. It takes two actions to load the weapon, two actions to aim it, and one action to fire it.

Name: The Ruby Legion

Nickname: The Red Legion, The Ruby Marauders, Gemstone Raiders, Bright Gems

Symbol: A ruby on a white field. Worn on clothing and displayed on shields.

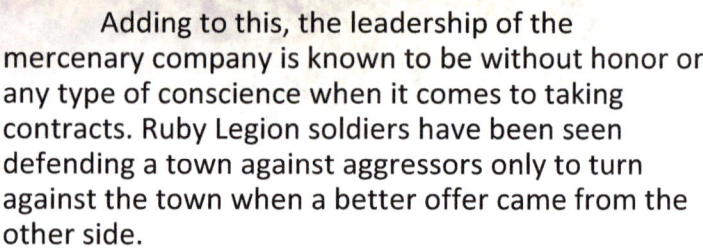

Type: Standing/Roaming

Size: Legion; 640/145

Cost: 2,400 gp/390 gp/185 gp per week

Leader: Octavio Romero de Medra (NE Human male †Spellknife 19)

Captains: 2; *Monica Hernan de Medra (NE Human female Fighter 16), Umbaro Akuna (N Human male Wizard 15)

Lieutenants: 12

Alignment: NE

Formation: The Ruby Legion fields an impressive 220 *light foot* with 150 *heavy foot* on the battlefield. A force of 60 *heavy mounted* serves as the cavalry while 30 *mercenary archers* and 50 *mounted skirmishers* prowl the lines looking for openings. Further complimenting the main units are 35 *mercenary acolytes* and 15 *mercenary priests*. The Legion sends 30 *mercenary ambushers* and 20 *spellknife ambushers* ahead of the main force to disrupt the enemy's lines. Magical might is considerable, with the company fielding 25 *mercenary wizards* and 5 *mercenary mages*.

Expertise: Guard Duty, Single/Sustained Battle, War

Trustworthiness: 3

Base: Ruby Towers; City-State of Medra (Verigal), Fort Umbral; Macehead Mountains (Verigal), Gemside Manor; City of Talis (Northern Savannah), Shadowtree Hall; Great Jungle

Sphere of Operations: Verigal (Esta, the Handle, Macehead, Northsea), Northern Savannah, Great Jungle

Government: Dictatorship

Tactics: The amount of soldiers the Ruby Legion can field at one time is impressive. Sometimes, just the sight of their soldiers forming ranks is enough to make the other side think twice about attacking.

Unfortunately, the discipline in the ranks is sub-par, and there have been times when the soldiers of the Legion have fled in the face of a superior enemy.

Adding to this, the leadership of the mercenary company is known to be without honor or any type of conscience when it comes to taking contracts. Ruby Legion soldiers have been seen defending a town against aggressors only to turn against the town when a better offer came from the other side.

Logistics: The Ruby Legion equips their soldiers with **average** arms and equipment. Many soldiers supplement their gear with a personal weapon, as well. The captains and lieutenants are decked out with magical weapons and armor; however, less than 20% of the soldiers will have some type of magic item.

History: The Ruby Legion was brought together by circumstances that led to the destruction of the City-State of Havor for breaching the City-State Pact. When the other city-states marched on Havor, thousands of mercenaries joined them for the promise of loot and glory. Among them was the fledgling company known as the Bright Gems, who were led by a young spellknife named Octavio Romero.

Octavio and his small band displayed great prowess during the battle, and it was the Bright Gems who were among the first attackers to storm the breach in Havor's walls. Hours later, the city fell, and its remaining inhabitants were placed in chains and marched out of the city. Octavio's charisma and combat expertise caused dozens of soldiers to leap at the opportunity to join the Bright Gems after the battle. Octavio even convinced two other companies to disband and join him. Thus, the Ruby Legion was born.

Elevated by his victory at Havor, Octavio was soon accepting contracts from numerous city-states and wealthy citizens. He constructed the Ruby Towers in his home city of Medra to act as the main headquarters for the growing mercenary company. Octavio used his considerable earnings to prolong his life through magic, but he is now ready to hand over operations to his hand-picked successor, Monica Hernan.

Notable NPCs: Spellknife Ambusher

†Spellknife described in *Manastorm: World of Shin'ar*

SPELLKNIFE AMBUSHER

Medium Humanoid (Human), NE

ARMOR CLASS
16 (scale mail)

HIT POINTS
30 (4d8+4)

SPEED
30 ft.

STR	DEX	CON	INT	WIS	CHA
14 (+2)	17 (+3)	13 (+1)	12 (+1)	12 (+1)	15 (+2)

SKILLS Acrobatics +5, Deception +4, Stealth +5

SENSES passive Perception 11

LANGUAGES Veri'urk, Tradespeech

CHALLENGE 2 (450 xp)

Heightened Evasion. If a spellknife ambusher makes a successful Dexterity saving throw against an attack that normally deals half damage on a successful save, they instead take no damage.

Sneak Attack. Once per turn, the spellknife ambusher deals an extra 7 (2d6) damage when it hits a target with a weapon attack and has *advantage* on the attack roll, or when the target is within 5 feet of an ally of the spellknife ambusher that isn't *incapacitated* and the spellknife ambusher does not have *disadvantage* on the attack roll.

Spellcasting. The spellknife ambusher is a level 4 spellcaster (DC 12, +4 to spell attacks).

Cantrips (at will): *blade ward, fire bolt, mage hand*

Level 1 (4 slots): *color spray, jump, thunderwave*

Level 2 (3 slots): *gust of wind, blur*

ACTIONS

Rapier. *Melee Weapon Attack*: +5 to hit, reach 5 ft.; One target. Hit: 8 (1d8+3) piercing damage.

Hand Crossbow. *Ranged Weapon Attack*: +5 to hit, range 30/120 ft.; One target. Hit: 7 (1d6+3) piercing damage.

EQUIPMENT

Scale mail, rapier, hand crossbow, crossbow bolt case with 20 bolts, mercenary pack, arcane focus

Name: The Silver Sellswords

Nickname: The Ragged Men, Twin-Swords

Symbol: Two swords, mirrored, on a white and red background. Flown on banners and flags and worn on surcoats.

Type: Recruiting/Fixed

Size: Regiment; 50 (260)/85

Cost: 700 gp/275 gp/100 gp per week

Leader: Sighvat Lundquist (N Human male Fighter 6/Bard 4)

Captains: 3; *Ivor Kellenson (LN Human male Fighter 9), Esmeralda Rocinni de Combra (CN Human female Sorcerer 11), Thrim Coldstare (N Frost Giant male)

Lieutenants: 4

Alignment: N

Formation: The Silver Sellswords' main force is comprised of 100 *light foot* and 50 *heavy foot*. They are accompanied by 15 *mercenary acolytes*, 5 *mercenary priests*, and 10 *mercenary sorcerers*. A force of 40 *mercenary archers* form up behind the ranks, and 30 *mercenary berserkers* are let loose to disrupt enemy formations. A unit of 10 *frost giant mercenaries* hurl boulders at oncoming foes and join melee combat if needed.

Expertise: Guard Duty, Single/Sustained Battle

Trustworthiness: 4

Base: Lundquist Manor; Barrowtown (Northern Tip)

Sphere of Operation: Northern Tip, Rusk Tribal Lands, Starfall Sea

Government: Military Council

Tactics: Making war in ten feet of snow has taught the Silver Sellswords a thing or two about adapting to the changing conditions of a battlefield. They excel at not only maneuverability but also in tenacity; the later-born from a life lived on the tundra of the Northern Tip.

The company takes all contracts, no matter how trivial, as long as their employer can pay. Sighvat Lundquist is one of the richest men in Barrowtown that is not affiliated with one of the town's crime families. Silver Sellswords are seen throughout the town, guarding homes and businesses against foul play.

Logistics: The Silver Sellswords outfit their soldiers with **average** arms and equipment. Sometimes known as the Ragged Men, many soldiers wear multiple layers of clothing to ward off the cold. Captains have numerous magical items, while the lieutenants and average soldier will most certainty have none. To supplement this, the company issues various potions to the soldiers before an upcoming battle.

History: The frozen fields of the Northern Tip are harsh and unforgiving. The type of people who make their home here reflects the brutality of the environment in their tempers and general demeanor. Simple arguments often lead to fights, which in turn lead to feuds. Amidst this rampant violence, one man saw the need for a professional fighting force that would dirty their hands for steady coin.

The Silver Sellswords were founded by Sighvat Lundquist shortly after he arrived in Barrowtown from the Kingdom of Jutan. At first, contracts came easy, guarding homes against theft and escorting caravans during the summer months to far off places such as Siimas and the Kingdom of the Flooded Forest.

The success of the company prompted numerous copycat outfits. Soon, the tundra became thick with hired swords, most of which were little more than back-alley killers, deemed too violent even for the Barrowtown crime families.

Despite the boom of mercenary work in the Northern Tip, the Silver Sellswords are still going strong, and are counted as one of the most dependable outfits in the region. Ten years ago, their ranks grew larger as Sighvat managed to hire a small group of Frost Giants from the clans that moved from their snowcapped homes to the valley floor in order to escape slavery at the hands of the Dragon siblings that conquered their home.

Notable NPCs: Frost Giant Mercenary

FROST GIANT MERCENARY
Huge Giant, NE

ARMOR CLASS
15 (half plate)
HIT POINTS
138 (12d12+60)
SPEED
40 ft.

STR 23 (+6)	DEX 09 (-1)	CON 21 (+5)	INT 09 (-1)	WIS 10 (+0)	CHA 12 (+1)

SAVING THROWS Constitution +8, Wisdom +3, Charisma +4
SKILLS Athletics +9, Perception +3
DAMAGE IMMUNITY Cold
SENSES passive Perception 13
LANGUAGES Giant
CHALLENGE 8 (3,900 xp)

Reckless Attack. The frost giant mercenary can choose to make their first attack on their turn recklessly, granting them *advantage* on melee weapon attack rolls using Strength, but attack rolls against them have *advantage* until their next turn.

ACTIONS

Multiattack. The frost giant mercenary can make two greataxe attacks.

Greataxe. *Melee Weapon Attack*: +9 to hit, reach 10 ft.; One target. Hit: 25 (3d12+6) slashing damage.

Rock. *Ranged Weapon Attack*: +9 to hit, range 60/240 ft.; One target. Hit: 28 (4d10+6) bludgeoning damage.

EQUIPMENT

Half plate, greataxe, sac with 15 throwing rocks, mercenary pack, a barrel of ale, sac of frozen meat

Name: Warriors of Light

Nickname: Lightbringers, Holy Legion

Symbol: A white star, often on a yellow or gold field. Worn on clothing and displayed on shields, but not flown on flags or pennants.

Type: Standing/Fixed

Size: Regiment; 340/70

Cost: 800 gp/290 gp/90 gp per week

Leader: Lucrecia Cusa de Bratasa (LG Human female Paladin 14)

Captains: 2; *Simon Boliv de Chaven (LG Human male Wizard 13), Zerachiel (LG Deva)

Lieutenants: 6

Alignment: LG

Formation: The Warriors of Light field 150 *light foot* and 50 *heavy foot* as their main combat force. They are supported by 40 *mercenary archers*, 20 *mercenary acolytes*, 15 *mercenary priests*, and 15 *mercenary wizards*. A force of 40 *mounted paladins* and 10 *Deva skirmishers* act as shock troops and often fight alongside the front line warriors.

Expertise: Single/Sustained Battle, War

Trustworthiness: 5

Base: Light's Hope (castle); City of Bratasa (Verigal)

Sphere of Operations: Verigal (Macehead, Northsea, Palous, Handle), Dark Sun Woods

Government: Military Council

Tactics: The Warriors of Light are keen to make sure their presence is felt on the battlefield. Always on the side of good and justice, the golden armored warriors stand impressive as their stalwart paladins parade up and down the ranks and their angelic comrades fly high above, inspiring the men with their mere presence.

Logistics: Soldiers are equipped with **above average** arms and armor. Potions and minor magical items that relate to protection are handed out to individual soldiers who earn them through valor and pious deeds.

History: The formation of the company comes from a disastrous time known as the Battle of Last Bastion. There, the Army of Light was decimated by a force of demons and devils, working together and worked up into a killing frenzy by some unknown entity. Thousands lost their lives that day, and many more were seen taken to the ruins of Libon to become slaves or sacrifices, and sometimes both. Those that did manage to escape the slaughter did so with little more than the clothes on their backs. They made their way west to the city of Bratasa, and what they thought was safety.

Because of the menace in which the refugees were fleeing, the gates to the city remained closed for fear the evil army would turn and march on the city for accepting those who escaped. Among the people were a handful of officers from the Army of Light who found themselves in charge of the fleeing masses. It was their voice, coupled with the shame in which their angelic allies brought upon the city's council that allowed the gates to open and the city to accept the refugees. Those officers went on to create a mercenary company from the remnant of the Army of Light that managed to escape that day of death.

21

DEVA SKIRMISHER

Medium Celestial, LG

ARMOR CLASS
17 (natural)

HIT POINTS
136 (16d8+64)

SPEED
30 ft.; Fly 90 ft.

STR 18 (+4) DEX 18 (+4) CON 18 (+4) INT 17 (+3) WIS 20 (+5) CHA 20 (+5)

SAVING THROWS
Wisdom +9, Charisma +9

SKILLS
Insight +9, Perception +9

DAMAGE RESISTANCE
Radiant; bludgeoning, piercing, and slashing from non-magical attacks

CONDITION IMMUNITIES
Charmed, exhaustion, frightened

SENSES
Darkvision 120 ft.; passive Perception 19

LANGUAGES
All, telepathy 120 ft.

CHALLENGE
10 (5,900 xp)

Angelic Weapons. The deva skirmisher's weapon attacks are magical. When the deva skirmisher hits with a weapon, the weapon deals an extra 4d8 radiant damage (included in the attack)

Battle Blessing. The deva skirmisher can use their reaction to grant a single ally within 30 feet of its position a +3 bonus to a one attack roll.

Innate Spellcasting. The deva skirmisher's spellcasting ability is Charisma (DC 17). They can innately cast the following spells, requiring only verbal components:

At will: *detect evil and good*

1/day each: *commune, raise dead*

Magic Resistance. The deva skirmisher has *advantage* on saving throws against spells and other magical effects.

ACTIONS

Multiattack. The deva skirmisher makes two melee attacks.

Spear. *Melee or Ranged Weapon Attack*: +8 to hit, reach 5 feet or 20/60 ft.; One target. Hit: 7 (1d6+4) piercing damage plus 18 (4d8) radiant damage.

Mace. *Melee Weapon Attack*: +8 to hit, reach 5 ft.; One target. Hit: 7 (1d6+4) bludgeoning damage plus 18 (4d8) radiant damage.

Healing Touch (3/day). The deva skirmisher touches another creature. The target magically regains 20 (4d8+2) hit points and is freed from any curse, disease, poison, blindness, or deafness.

Change Shape. The deva skirmisher magically polymorphs into a humanoid or beast that has a CR equal to or less than its own, or back into its true form. The deva retains its game stats and ability to speak, but its AC, movement modes, Strength, Dexterity, and any special senses are replaced by those of the new form.

EQUIPMENT

Spear, mace, holy symbol, pouch of polished stones (gifts for children)

Name: The Winged Brotherhood

Nickname: The Birds of War, Birdmen, The Winged Crusaders

Symbol: An eagle with its wings splayed on a red and blue background. Worn on clothing, but never flown from flags.

Type: Standing/Roaming

Size: Regiment; 260/40

Cost: 780 gp/300 gp/100 gp per week

Leader: Milad Namdar (CG Aravork male †Aerialist 6/Sorcerer 5)

Captains: 2; *Omar Gul (CG Aravork make Ranger 11), Vanda Resi (CG Aravork female Aerialist 9)

Lieutenants: 4

Alignment: CG

Formation: The Winged Brotherhood has 95 *light foot,* and 75 *heavy foot* form up their ranks with 15 *mercenary acolytes* and 20 *mercenary sorcerers* supporting them. A force of 55 *aerialist ambushers* stay airborne as much as possible, picking off enemies with precise arrow fire.

Expertise: Single/Sustained Battle, War

Trustworthiness: 4

Base: Tower of Phoenix Fire; Orath-Aerie, Tower of Flame; The Bleek (outside Farhome)

Sphere of Operations: Verigal (Esta, Handle, Macehead), Northern Savannah, The Bleek

Government: Brotherhood Clan

Tactics: Perhaps the most well-known tactic of the Winged Brotherhood is its ability to field so many flying units. Groups of Aravork soldiers take to the air at a moment's notice, crashing down on their adversaries with near-suicidal dives. Peppering the enemy ranks with concentrated arrow fire and thrown explosives, the Winged Brotherhood never manages to disappoint their clients with their tenacity and aerial acrobatics.

The company is a huge supporter of the "Return" movement among individual Aravork clans. They see themselves as instrumental in helping their people regain territory on the Southern Continent that was lost to them so long ago. They never take contracts that pit them against Aravork or Calvoid communities.

Logistics: The Winged Brotherhood outfits their soldiers in **average** equipment. It is worth noting that every soldier, even front line combatants, are issued a ranged weapon and ammunition. Captains and lieutenants are decked out in magical armor and many sport magical weapons as well. Roughly 22% of soldiers will have a personal common or uncommon magic item.

History: In Aravork communities, an Aerialist is a hero and one who the young aspire to be. The training it takes to become the race's famed aerial warriors is rigorous, and one in five do not pass the final test to earn the title of Aerialist.

Milad Namdar was head of his graduating class, a pupil who not only took what he learned and applied it but was intelligent enough to improvise at a moment's notice. He rose quickly through the ranks of Migratory Guards, volunteering for missions whenever he could. He traveled far and met and befriended many Aravork around the planet. When it came time to retire, he used his connections to put together a mercenary company made up of elite soldiers, many of whom served with Milad in Migratory Guard units.

Applying what all of his knowledge of airborne warfare, Milad built a fighting force that quickly earned a reputation for not only trustworthiness but for their unique abilities and fighting technique. Hails of arrows and pin-cushioned corpses are their calling card.

Notable NPCs: Aerialist Ambusher

†Aerialist described in Manastorm: World of Shin'ar

AERIALIST AMBUSHER

Medium Humanoid (Aravork), Any alignment

ARMOR CLASS
16 (studded leather)

HIT POINTS
23 (4d8)

SPEED
30 ft.; Fly 60 ft.

STR 12 (+1)	DEX 18 (+4)	CON 11 (+0)	INT 10 (+0)	WIS 12 (+1)	CHA 11 (+0)

SKILLS Acrobatics +6, Stealth +6
SENSES passive Perception 11
LANGUAGES Avar'urk, Tradespeech
CHALLENGE 1 (200 xp)

Aerial Evasion. While airborne, when the aerialist ambusher is forced to make a Dexterity saving throw against an attack that normally deals half damage on a successful save, they instead take no damage.

Death From Above. Once per turn, the aerialist ambusher can deal an extra 7 (2d6) weapon damage with a ranged weapon if they have *advantage* on the attack roll or if another enemy of the target is within 5 feet of it and that enemy isn't *incapacitated*. The aerialist ambusher must be either airborne or at least 40 feet above their target, as well.

ACTIONS

Shortbow. Ranged Weapon Attack: +6 to hit, range 80/320 ft.; One target. Hit: 9 (1d8+4) piercing damage.

Shortsword. Melee Weapon Attack: +6 to hit, reach 5 ft.; One target. Hit: 8 (1d6+4) piercing damage.

EQUIPMENT

Studded leather armor, shortsword, shortbow, quiver with 40 arrows, mercenary pack

CHAPTER TWO
REGIONAL COMPANIES

Name: Alonzo's Hammers

Nickname: The Hammers

Symbol: An argent warhammer on a red background. Flown on flags and displayed on shields.

Type: Standing/Fixed

Size: Troop; 58/10

Cost: 300 gp/130 gp/50 gp per week

Leader: Alonzo Romero de Fatera (N Human male Fighter 8)

Captains: 1; *Alii *vas* Trondon (N Calvoid female Wizard 8)

Lieutenants: 3

Alignment: N

Formation: The Hammers field 30 *light foot* and 20 *heavy foot* as their main fighting force. Mixed into those units, you will find 5 *mercenary acolytes* and 3 *mercenary wizards*.

Expertise: Guard Duty, Single/Sustained Battle

Trustworthiness: 4

Base: Hammerhall; City-State of Fatera (Verigal)

Sphere of Operation: Verigal (Sylvar)

Government: Dictatorship

Tactics: Alonzo's Hammers form close ranks on the battlefield. Drills and mandatory arms practice are held every day when not engaged in a contract. The company excels in small unit tactics, and one of their favorite maneuvers is breaking into tightly packed 15 man squads that move about the battlefield in perfect coordination.

Alonzo insists on negotiating every contract himself, and he is not an easy man to speak with. His brash personality has not won him many friends; however, he is well known for his business sense, and he has parlayed the gold his company earns into lucrative ventures.

Logistics: The Hammers are equipped with **average** arms and armor. Alonzo does not let his soldiers fight in unkept equipment, though he also does not shell out top coin for higher quality arms either.

His captain and lieutenants will have numerous magical items, and potions are distributed to front line combatants before large engagements. There is an 18% chance the average soldier will have a personal magic item or common or uncommon value.

History: The Hammer's started as an adventuring company headed by Alonzo's brother, Malo Romero. After six years exploring ruins and selling their talents to the highest bidder, Malo retired to Fatera and opened up an inn. Alonzo, not ready to give up the thrill of battle, enlisted his good friend Alii *vas* Trondon to help him establish a small, but well trained mercenary company.

Contracts came quickly, as the Romero brothers built a reputation for their combat skills and intelligence on the battlefield. Because of their smaller size, the company deals mostly with guarding caravans and dignitaries as they travel around the Sylvar province of Verigal.

Name: The Blackhearts

Nickname: The Shadowmen, Shadow Soldiers

Symbol: An upside-down black heart on a white field, often accompanied by a fanged skull. Flown on flags but almost never worn on clothing or armor.

Type: Standing/Fixed

Size: Battalion; 75/10

Cost: 400 gp/200 gp/60 gp per week

Leader: Telone Azzuddin (NE Drampyr male †Shadowgiest 12)

Captains: 2; *Fazil Darkeyes (NE Drampyr male Rogue 11), Annette Inez de Eltra-Menco (NE Human female Sorcerer 9)

Lieutenants: 2

Alignment: NE

Formation: The Blackhearts main force is comprised of 25 *light foot* and 15 *heavy foot*. A unit of 5 *mercenary priests* and 10 *mercenary sorcerers* back up the front lines while 20 *shadowgiest skirmishers* roam the battlefield disrupting enemy lines and dealing out quick-strike attacks.

Expertise: Single/Sustained Battle

Trustworthiness: 2

†Shadowgiest described in Manastorm: World of Shin'ar

Base: Blackstone Tower; Eltra-Menco (Verigal)

Sphere of Operations: Verigal (Palous)

Government: Dictatorship

Tactics: The Blackhearts use a mixture of magical and martial might while on the battlefield. A favored tactic is softening up the enemy with coordinated attacks by the unit of shadowgiest skirmishers coupled with a magical onslaught from the company's sorcerers. The foot soldiers move in and mop up whatever is left.

The company is not picky when choosing contracts. Most of their coin comes from the wealthy Eltrabi, who have made their home in Verigal, as well as humans who have little in the way or moral fortitude. They are often paid to raid caravans and to conduct sneak attacks against their employer's rivals.

Logistics: The Blackhearts have **average** arms and armor. The captains and lieutenants will have a number of magical items, mostly pertaining to stealth or darkness related magic. Around 31% of the average soldiers will have a personal common or uncommon magical item or weapon.

History: When the town of Menco was split, and the northern half was given over to Eltrabi rule, the wealthy vampire-kin brought with them numerous servants and retainers to help establish their households. Among them were a cadre of shadowgiest who swore allegiance to House Azzuddin. The elite group of shadow conjuring warriors helped secure a place for their masters through assassinations and intimidation tactics against the human population. After a decade of internal strife, the simmering aggression between the townspeople died down, and something of a normal life was resumed by the town's inhabitants.

The young scion of House Azzuddin and his best friend formed the Blackhearts from the bored offspring of the Eltrabi, who co-ruled the town. It was years before the company accepted human members, but now the group is comprised of roughly 70% Eltrabi and 30% Vergal. Those who fight under the blackheart banner are welcomed in Eltra-Menco but are forbidden from entering other Verigal settlements. This keeps the small company close to home, where there is no shortage of contracts to fulfill.

Notable NPCs: Shadowgiest Skirmisher

SHADOWGIEST SKIRMISHER

Medium Humanoid (Drampyr), NE

ARMOR CLASS
15 (studded leather)

HIT POINTS
30 (4d8+8)

SPEED
30 ft.

STR 14 (+2) DEX 17 (+3) CON 14 (+2) INT 10 (+0) WIS 10 (+0) CHA 12 (+1)

SKILLS Acrobatics +5, Perception +2, Stealth +5

SENSES Darkvision 60 ft., passive Perception 12

LANGUAGES Eltra'urk, Tradespeech

CHALLENGE 1 (200 xp)

Eidolon. The shadowgiest skirmisher can conjure a shadow minion to fight on their behalf. They can conjure the minion using their action and dismiss the minion using a bonus action. The minion uses the shadowgiest's bonus action to attack or move.

Sneak Attack. Once per turn, the shadowgiest skirmisher deals an extra 7 (2d6) damage when it hits a target with a weapon attack and has *advantage* on the attack roll, or when the target is within 5 feet of an ally of the shadowgiest skirmisher that isn't *incapacitated* and the shadowgiest skirmisher does not have *disadvantage* on the attack roll.

ACTIONS

Rapier. Melee Weapon Attack: +5 to hit, reach 5 ft.; One target. Hit: 8 (1d8+3) piercing damage.

Dagger. Melee or Ranged Weapon Attack: +5 to hit, reach 5 feet, or range 20/60 ft.; One target. Hit: 6 (1d4+3) piercing damage.

Hand Crossbow. Ranged Weapon Attack: +5 to hit, range 30/120 ft.; One target. Hit: 7 (1d6+3) piercing damage.

EQUIPMENT

Studded leather armor, rapier, 2 daggers, hand crossbow, crossbow bolt case with 20 crossbow bolts, mercenary pack

SHADOW MINION

Medium Monstrosity, NE

ARMOR CLASS
17 (natural)
HIT POINTS
30 (4d8+8)
SPEED
30 ft.

STR 14 (+2) DEX 17 (+3) CON 14 (+2) INT 10 (+0) WIS 10 (+0) CHA 12 (+1)

SKILLS Acrobatics +5, Perception +2, Stealth +5

SENSES Darkvision 60 ft., passive Perception 12

LANGUAGES Understands any language their master can speak, but they cannot speak

CHALLENGE ½ (100 xp)

Evolutions. The shadow minion's reach is extended by 5 feet, and it has dagger-like claws.

Incorporeal Strikes. The shadow minion's melee attacks affect incorporeal creatures as if they were corporal.

Spell Immunity. The shadow minion is unaffected by *dispel magic*.

ACTIONS

Claws. Melee Weapon Attack: +5 to hit, reach 10 ft.; One target. Hit: 7 (1d6+3) necrotic damage.

Name: The Gray Riders

Nickname: The Swift Riders

Symbol: Three gray horse heads, conjoined, on a brown or white field. Displayed on shields and barding.

Type: Standing/Fixed

Size: Troop; 45/10

Cost: 300 gp/180 gp/60 gp per week

Leader: Petula Ibori (N Human female Fighter 10)

Captains: 1; *Anatoli Akuna (N Human male Ranger 8)

Lieutenants: 3

Alignment: N

Formation: The Gray Riders field 20 *mounted skirmishers*, 10 *heavy mounted*, and 10 *mercenary priests* as their main attacking force. A small unit of 5 *mercenary wizards* pitches in where they can. All of the Gray Riders are mounted.

Expertise: Single/Sustained Battle

Trustworthiness: 4

Base: Fort Farasi; Northern Savannah

Sphere of Operation: Northern Savannah

Government: Council

Tactics: The Gray Riders send in their mounted skirmishers first to disrupt the enemy's lines. When a break forms, the heavy mounted charge and exploit it. Each soldier in the company is issued their own horse to ride into battle. The soldiers care for their own horses in camp and sometimes spend their earnings on embellishing their individual saddles and barding to make them stand out in battle.

Petula Ibori is a shrewd tactician. She is an expert at mounted combat, and she and her council make sure each soldier in the company is as familiar riding a horse as they are walking on their own two feet.

Logistics: The soldiers of the Gray Riders are given **above average** weapons and gear. Petula has less magical items for a woman of her stature than you would think, but she is known to hand out minor magical items to soldiers who earn her respect on the battlefield. Because of this, almost 50% of her soldiers will have a personal common or uncommon magic item, weapon, or suit of armor.

History: The Gray Riders began as an experiment, of sorts. A group of wealthy horse dealers was looking for new revenue streams when they were introduced to Petula Ibori.

The combat veteran impressed them with her knowledge of horse breeds and temperaments. They went on to bankroll the formation of the Gray Riders, with Petula calling the shots. She quickly enlisted the help of her lifelong friend Anatoli Akuna, and they set about selecting the most excellent riders in the Northern Savannah to make up the first soldiers of their new company.

The group of traders was paid back their initial investment quickly, plus some extra coin to buy out their stakes in the mercenary company. Petula, along with her council of veterans, now owns and funds the company themselves. They continue to see success on the battlefield thanks to their superior tactics and pension for well-coordinated cavalry charges.

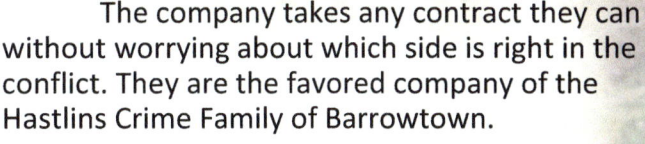

Name: Redhawk's Reavers
Nickname: Red Birds, Bloody Birds
Symbol: A red hawk, perched, on a black and argent field. The symbol is displayed on shields but never worn or flown.
Type: Standing/Fixed
Size: Battalion; 70/15
Cost: 400 gp/130 gp/90 gp per week
Leader: The Redhawk (CE Human male Barbarian 6/Ranger 6)
Captains: 1; *Tenna of the White Wyrm (CE Rusk male Barbarian 9)
Lieutenants: 3
Alignment: CE
Formation: The Reavers field an impressive 50 *mercenary berserkers* on the battlefield, accompanied by 10 *mercenary acolytes* and 10 *white wyrm skirmishers*.
Expertise: Single/Sustained Battle
Trustworthiness: 2
Base: Redhawk's Cage (manor house); Barrowtown
Sphere of Operations: Seal Point
Government: Dictatorship
Tactics: The Bloody Birds have little in the way of combat tactics. Mostly, they just form up loose lines and charge at the enemy when told to do so. The Rusk skirmishers are sometimes sent in first to disrupt enemy positions if the enemy force looks like it contains more disciplined troops then the Reavers are used to facing.

The company takes any contract they can without worrying about which side is right in the conflict. They are the favored company of the Hastlins Crime Family of Barrowtown.

Logistics: The company provides **poor** arms and equipment to its soldiers. The Redhawk is very wealthy but hoards his coin like a dragon. He does pay his soldiers a good wage, but not out of the goodness in his heart, but rather so they don't revolt and kill him in his sleep. The average soldier in the company will have a 10% chance to own a common or uncommon magical item.

History: The Redhawk came to the Northern Tip from the Kingdom of Jutan almost two decades ago. Fleeing what he describes as persecution for his faith, he established himself in and around Barrowtown as a hired killer and wilderness guide. While escorting a delegation of Hastlin Family merchants through Rusk Tribal Lands, they were attacked by a group of marauding White Wyrm tribesmen. The Redhawk single-handedly slew four Rusk before the rest of the party drove off the savages. Impressed with his ferocity, the fleeing tribesmen vowed to remember his name.

Three years later, the Redhawk was again in Rusk Tribal Lands near the southern edge of the Ice Scale Woods. He was ambushed by a Rusk raiding party, but before he was to be killed, the leader of the party called for a parlay. It turns out that Rusk was among the marauders who fled from the Redhawk all those years ago. He gave Redhawk a choice, beat him in unarmed combat, or die that day. The Redhawk gladly accepted and went on the defeat the Rusk, whose name was Tenna, after a brutal one hour fight. Both combatants were exhausted and near death, but the win gave Redhawk more prestige in the eyes of the assembled Rusk. He was let go and told he could call on Tenna anytime for another fight.

Redhawk took Tenna up on that offer less than nine months later when he returned to the southern Ice Scale Woods with a proposal. The Reavers were formed that day, and Tenna and his war band left the safety of their tribe to fight alongside the Redhawk for gold and glory.

Notable NPCs: White Wyrm Skirmisher

WHITE WYRM SKIRMISHER

Medium Humanoid (Rusk), CE

ARMOR CLASS
13 (hide)
HIT POINTS
44 (4d10+16)
SPEED
25 ft.

STR 18 (+4) DEX 12 (+1) CON 18 (+4) INT 09 (-1) WIS 10 (+0) CHA 09 (-1)

SKILLS Animal Handling +2, Nature +1
DAMAGE RESISTANCE Cold
SENSES Darkvision 60 ft., passive Perception 10
LANGUAGES Ruskivan
CHALLENGE 2 (450 xp)

Animalistic Rage. Whenever the white wyrm skirmisher takes the attack action, they enter an animalistic rage that increases their melee weapon damage by 2 points, grants them resistance to bludgeoning, piercing, and slashing damage, and gives them *advantage* on Strength saving throws and ability checks. The rage ends if they ever have a turn where they don't take the attack action.

Totemic Bond. The white wyrm skirmisher is bonded to a white dragyl, which guards and fights for the skirmisher. The dragyl uses its own initiative count and can be given orders (no action needed) by the white wyrm skirmisher. If no action is given, the dragyl will defend itself and its master from harm.

ACTIONS

Greataxe. *Melee Weapon Attack*: +6 to hit, reach 5 ft.; One target. Hit: 11 (1d12+4) slashing damage.

Javelin. *Melee or Ranged Weapon Attack*: +6 to hit, reach 5 feet, or range 30/120 ft.; One target. Hit: 8 (1d6+4) piercing damage.

EQUIPMENT

Hide armor, greataxe, 6 javelins, mercenary pack, sac of frozen meat (food for dragyl)

YOUNG WHITE DRAGYL

Small Beast (Dragyl), CE

ARMOR CLASS
15 (natural)
HIT POINTS
27 (3d12+6)
SPEED
30 ft.

STR 12 (+1) DEX 12 (+1) CON 14 (+2) INT 05 (-3) WIS 12 (+1) CHA 14 (+2)

SKILLS Perception +2, Stealth +1
DAMAGE IMMUNITY Cold
SENSES passive Perception 13
LANGUAGES Understands Ruskivan and Draconic but cannot speak
CHALLENGE 2 (450 xp)

Keen Senses. The white dragyl gains a +3 bonus to Wisdom (Perception) checks that rely on scent.

ACTIONS

Multiattack. The white dragyl can make two claw attacks, one bite and one claw attack, or a slam attack followed by a bite. It can also choose to use its breath weapon if it is available in place of any one attack.

Bite. Melee Weapon Attack: +3 to hit, reach 5 ft.; One target. Hit: 5 (1d6+1) piercing damage.

Claw. Melee Weapon Attack: +3 to hit, reach 5 ft.; One target. Hit: 4 (1d4+1) slashing damage.

Slam. Melee Weapon Attack: +3 to hit, reach 5 ft.; One target. Hit: 5 (1d6+1) bludgeoning damage.

Breath Weapon (2/day). The young white dragyl can exhale a 20-foot cone of frost that deals 6 (1d10) cold damage to any creature who fails a DC 12 Dexterity saving throw or half damage on a successful saving throw.

Name: Redya's Company

Nickname: The Red Cats

Symbol: A red stylized feline face on a black background. Worn on shields and displayed on clothing.

Type: Standing/Fixed

Size: Battalion; 105/20

Cost: 300 gp/200 gp/75 gp per week

Leader: Redya Yodha (N Kalarin female Fighter 12)

Captains: 2; *Kamu Anadi (N Kalarin male †Geomancer 11), Hana Rao (NG Kalarin female Wizard 7)

Lieutenants: 2

Alignment: N

Formation: Red's Company fields 70 *light foot* and 20 *mercenary archers*. A small unit of 5 *mercenary acolytes* accompanies them in battle. In front of the main force, a group consisting of 5 *geomancer ambushers* and 5 *mercenary ambushers* are sent in to disrupt enemy lines.

Expertise: Guard Duty, Single/Sustained Battle

Trustworthiness: 3

Base: Red's Manor; Siimas (Starfall Sea)

Sphere of Operations: Starfall Sea

Government: Counseled Dictatorship

Tactics: Redya's Company can seem disorganized at times. The front ranks form up tightly, at first, but they have been known to break ranks when the battle is joined. Individual soldiers try for personal glory, a common Kalarin practice, even if it goes against their superior's wishes.

Redya punishes those who try and win personal glory and end up hurting the company's efforts. However, those who break ranks and somehow not only survive but help win the day, are showered with praise and coin.

Redya has never reneged on a contract, and the company's trustworthiness would reflect this if not for the vicious lies told about her by her competitors. Such things have, in the past, hurt her company's reputation.

Logistics: The company is outfitted with **average** arms and equipment. Because of the infrequency that they get contracts, coin is sometimes in short supply. Most of her soldiers are exiled and runaway Kalarin who are used to living poorly, so the lean times do not affect them as much as you would think.

Red and her captains have numerous magical items between them, and she is known to gift minor magic to her soldiers. Roughly 25% of the company will have a personal common or uncommon magical item or weapon.

History: Redya Yodha was born Wafa Lanka, the eldest daughter of a Raja and his favorite wife. She grew up in the lap of luxury, often dining with foreign dignitaries and prominent officials. She was intelligent and athletic and longed to become a famous warrior like her father. Unfortunately, the social hierarchy of her homeland forbids women from advancing in the military. She began to teach herself swordplay in secret, even dressing as a man and entering underground fighting clubs. On one such occasion, after defeating three warriors at once, she was found out and arrested. Only her family name kept her from the headsman's block. She chose exile to keep her family name intact.

She arrived in Siimas, a place where many exiled Kalarin has migrated to since the reopening of the Kala Dominion to outsiders. In that predominately human city, she was able to practice arms in public, and quickly earned a reputation as a sellsword. Her many exploits helped her when it came time to form her company. She accepted any exiled Kalarin who wished to join, male or female. The social norms the genders must adhere to in her native county are not followed by her or her company.

Notable NPCs: Geomancer Ambusher

†*Geomancer described in Manastorm: World of Shin'ar*

GEOMANCER AMBUSHER

Medium Humanoid (Kalarin), Any alignment

ARMOR CLASS
15 (unarmored)

HIT POINTS
30 (4d8+8)

SPEED
40 ft.

STR	DEX	CON	INT	WIS	CHA
14 (+2)	17 (+3)	14 (+2)	12 (+1)	14 (+2)	15 (+2)

SKILLS Acrobatics +5, Stealth +5
SENSES Darkvision 60 ft., passive Perception 12

LANGUAGES Kaliv, Tradespeech
CHALLENGE 1 (200 xp)

Martial Arts. The geomancer ambusher deals 1d4 slashing damage with unarmed attacks. In addition, they can make a single unarmed attack as a bonus action.

Spellcasting. The geomancer ambusher is a level 4 spellcaster (DC 12, +4 to spell attacks).

Cantrips (at will): acid splash, fire bolt, mage hand, mending, shocking grasp

Level 1 (4 slots): chromatic orb, color spray, fog cloud

Level 2 (3 slots): blur, scorching ray

Unarmed Defense. While wearing no armor, the geomancer ambusher has an AC equal to 10 + Dexterity modifier + Wisdom modifier.

ACTIONS

Unarmed Attack. Melee Weapon Attack: +5 to hit, reach 5 ft.; One target. Hit: 6 (1d4+3) slashing damage.

Shortbow. Ranged Weapon Attack: +5 to hit, range 80/320 ft.; One target. Hit: 7 (1d6+3) piercing damage.

EQUIPMENT

Shortbow, quiver with 20 arrows, mercenary pack

Name: The Sapphire Guard
Nickname: The Blue Helms
Symbol: A sapphire gem on a white field. Flown on flags and worn on clothing. All foot soldiers wear blue colored helms.
Type: Recruiting/Fixed
Size: Brigade; 50 (100)/45
Cost: 450 gp/200 gp/85 gp per week
Leader: Commander Cyril Lissouba (N Human male Fighter 17)
Captain: 1; *Oliyad Baffour (LN Human male Monk 15)
Lieutenants: 4
Alignment: N
Formation: The Sapphire Guard forms up 110 *light foot* and 55 *heavy foot* as their front line combatants. They are accompanied by 40 *mercenary archers*, 10 *mercenary wizards*, and 15 *mercenary acolytes*. A small force of 20 o*gre shield-breakers* acts as powerful vanguard troops.
Expertise: Guard Duty, Single/Sustained Battle
Trustworthiness: 4
Base: Tower of Sapphires; Tiagba (Golden Coast)
Sphere of Operation: Golden Coast
Government: Military
Tactics: The Sapphire Guard's main tactic is to form up to three ranks of foot soldiers, each slightly staggered off the next. The archers, wizards, and acolytes fill in any gaps. The ogres are deployed first if it looks like the enemy is better organized then reports would suggest. Very few shield walls stand up to twenty ogres in plate mail running at full speed.

Commander Lissouba is honorable and is known to adhere to a contract's terms. He is a shrewd negotiator and often talks an employer into giving bonus coins to his troops for bravery.

Logistics: The company has **above average** equipment. The pay the ordinary soldier gains with the Sapphire Guard is twice as much as other companies in the region; however, the Sapphire Guard is very picky on who they allow to wear a blue helm. Most of the recruited troops come from a list of past veterans, or their kin. The company feels like an extended family for many of the soldiers.

Commander Lissouba has countless magical items, and around 30% of his troops will have a common or uncommon magical item.

Each soldier is issued a *potion of healing* upon signing up, and they can purchase additional potions at a discount from the company's supplies.

History: The Sapphire Guard started out as an extension of the town of Tiagba's guard. The settlement entered into an agreement with the Empire of Alteria that stated they could have no more than one city guardsmen per two hundred and fifty inhabitants, which left the town willfully unprotected.

To get around this, the town council enlisted the aid of a well-liked war hero and funded the formation of a mercenary company run by him. Cyril Lissouba declined at first, as he was enjoying his retirement, but he saw the need for the town to be adequately protected.

The company's first contract was to man and defend the town's new walls. Years would pass, and the Sapphire Guard became synonymous with the protection of the town of Tiagba. So much so that foreign merchants think they are, in fact, the town's municipal watch.

The company has taken other contracts over the years. They saw much combat in the south when the settlement of Rodisa hired them to quell an ogre uprising on their eastern border. The Sapphire Guard displayed such prowess during that campaign that the ogre tribes in that area surrendered after two battles. One tribe would go as far as enter a pact with Commander Lissouba and join the ranks of the company when needed.

Recently, the company has been seen in the Zagos Mountains scouting tunnel systems that seemed to appear out of nowhere overnight. Both the city of Rodisa and Tiagba are concerned that the Stazi ant-people are moving west since they have been repeatedly rebuked from their incursions into the Great Jungle far to the east.

Notable NPCs: Ogre Shield-breaker

OGRE SHIELD-BREAKER

Large Giant, N

ARMOR CLASS
20 (plate mail, shield)

HIT POINTS
59 (7d10+21)

SPEED
40 ft.

STR	DEX	CON	INT	WIS	CHA
19 (+4)	08 (-1)	16 (+3)	08 (-1)	08 (-1)	08 (-1)

SENSES Darkvision 60 ft., passive Perception 09

LANGUAGES Giant

CHALLENGE 3 (700 xp)

Charge. If the ogre shield-breaker moves at least 30 feet straight toward a target and then hits it with a melee weapon attack on the same turn, the target takes an extra 15 (3d8) damage from the force of the blow.

ACTIONS

Morningstar. Melee Weapon Attack: +6 to hit, reach 5 ft.; One target. Hit: 9 (1d8+4) piercing damage.

EQUIPMENT

Plate mail, shield, morningstar, mercenary pack, sac of soiled rags, broken shield-piece necklace

Name: The Swift Blades

Nickname: The Quick Blades, The Silver Blades

Symbol: Two argent crossed swords, on a blue or yellow field. Worn on clothing and displayed on shields.

Type: Standing/Fixed

Size: Battalion; 100/25

Cost: 380 gp/200 gp/60 gp per week

Leader: Sofia Rubio de Hortta (N Human female Fighter 12)

Captains: 2; *Muric Ortez de Hortta (NE Human male Spellknife 9), Josepha Rubio de Hortta (NE Human female Warlock 8)

Lieutenants: 4

Alignment: N

Formation: The Swift Blades field 50 *light foot* and 10 *heavy foot*. A force of 10 *mercenary acolytes* and 5 *mercenary sorcerers* are filtered into the front ranks. When deception is called for, 10 *mercenary ambushers* and 15 *mercenary archers* are deployed to harass enemy positions.

Expertise: Single/Sustained Battle

Trustworthiness: 3

Base: Swift-blade Hall; City-State of Hortta (Verigal)

Sphere of Operations: Verigal (Esta)

Government: Dictatorship

Tactics: The Swift Blades employ typical tactics when engaging with an enemy force. The foot soldiers line up and move in a coordinated step while the sorcerers and archers soften the opposition from behind the ranks.

Sofia Rubio is as abrasive as it gets, and she does not negotiate contracts for her company. Instead, she relies on her little sister, Josepha, to do the talking for her. Sofia is often found passed out, drunk, in the soldier barracks. She refuses to drink while out on campaign, and her sister makes sure she keeps that promise.

Logistics: The company issues **average** arms and equipment to their soldiers. Potions are in ready supply, and a number of them are given to soldiers before important battles. Sofia and her sister have accumulated numerous magical items over the years, and she is known to gift them to soldiers who prove their worth to her.

She is also known to use magic items to bet on rounds of *Chinchon*, a popular Vergal card game. She is a horrible gambler and a notorious drunk, so she loses more times than she wins. Because of this, almost 50% of her soldiers will have some kind of personal common or uncommon magical item or weapon.

History: Sofia and her sister were born to the wealthy Rubio family in the City-State of Hortta. The family's money came mostly from shipping, but supporting pirates was their most lucrative venture. Sofia ran away from home at the age of sixteen to join a pirate crew. She came back a few weeks later after she learned she gets terribly seasick. Instead of punishing her, her parents instead sent her to live and train with a well-known swordsmen. She excelled in swordplay and made quite a name for herself in the city's fighting pits and arenas.

Never one to rest on her success, she parlayed the coin she earned being a prize-fighter and professional duelist into forming a mercenary company. She enlisted the aid of her younger sister and her best friend, Muric, to help her run the company. Contracts came quickly and often. Soon, the Swift Blades were seen all over the province, fighting bandits and raiding caravans themselves, at the behest of their employers.

Sofia's many vices have endangered the well-being of the company on several occasions. She would show up to the battle, drunk, or hung over, and her sister would always have to cover for her. After a particularly disastrous defeat at the hands of the Brotherhood of the Shining Shield, she vowed to never drink while fulfilling a contract again.

CHAPTER THREE
SPECIALIZED COMPANIES

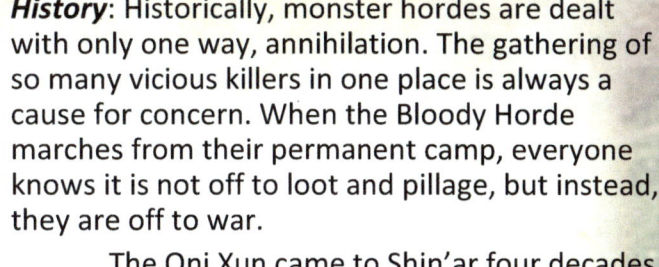

Name: The Bloody Horde

Nickname: The Horde

Symbol: Two stylized oni heads on a red and white checked background. Flown on flags but never worn or displayed.

Type: Standing/Fixed

Size: Brigade; 200/25

Cost: 300 gp/100 gp/60 gp per week

Leader: Xun (LE male Oni)

Captains: 2; *Aiko (LE female Oni), Grimbok (CE male Bugbear Chief)

Lieutenants: 2

Alignment: LE

Formation: The Horde typically masses 90 *mercenary goblins* backed by 35 *mercenary bugbears* as their main attacking force. A large unit of 75 *kobold ambushers* is sent ahead of the main group to deplete the enemy's numbers before engagement.

Expertise: Single/Sustained Battle, War

Trustworthiness: 3

Base: Permanent camp; Haunted Forest (The Bleek)

Sphere of Operations: The Bleek, Dark Sun Woods, Verigal (Macehead)

Government: Dictatorship

Tactics: Most who face the Horde do not expect any type of brilliant military tactics. They are often surprised when the seemingly poorly equipped force forms up perfect ranks. Drills are constant back at their camp, and the bugbear troops make sure the other soldiers stay in line.

Xun and his partner Aiko negotiate every contract together. Aiko is smarter than her husband; however, Xun has a multitude of contacts from his own days as a mercenary in the war-torn fields of Verigal.

Logistics: The Bloody Horde is outfitted with **poor** arms and equipment. Xun and his command staff have many magical items and weapons between them, but the average soldier will have next to none.

History: Historically, monster hordes are dealt with only one way, annihilation. The gathering of so many vicious killers in one place is always a cause for concern. When the Bloody Horde marches from their permanent camp, everyone knows it is not off to loot and pillage, but instead, they are off to war.

The Oni Xun came to Shin'ar four decades ago when he fell through an open portal on his home planet. He found himself stranded on an alien world, though it was not too dissimilar from his own. After wondering for a few weeks, he came upon a forest covered in snow. Numerous clans of Goblinoids and other monsters clashed over the limited resources to be found in the woods and surrounding tundra.

Xun conquered a mid-sized goblin tribe and used them as fodder to take over a large section of territory in the eastern woods. From here, he began a campaign of lies and deceit to win over the loyalty of a kobold clan who were also newcomers to the planet. As his ranks grew, so did his reputation as a being of intellect and wit.

He would often leave his forest home to travel south, to the human cities of Verigal. There, he found work as a mercenary, lending his talents to numerous companies whose morality was lacking just enough to hire an eight-foot blue-skinned ogre.

Learning what he could from his time in Verigal, Xun returned to his home and began teaching his subjects combat techniques and battlefield formations. Soon, the Bloody Horde was born, and he began taking contracts wherever he could find them.

Notable NPCs: Mercenary Goblin,

MERCENARY GOBLIN

Small Humanoid (Goblinoid), NE

ARMOR CLASS

15 (padded armor, shield)

HIT POINTS

11 (2d6+4)

SPEED

30 ft.

STR 08 (-1) DEX 14 (+2) CON 10 (+0) INT 10 (+0) WIS 08 (-1) CHA 08 (-1)

SKILLS Stealth +6

SENSES Darkvision 60 ft., passive Perception 09

LANGUAGES Goblinoid

CHALLENGE ½ (100 xp)

Battle Tested. Mercenary goblins gain a +2 bonus to saving throws to resist the *frightened* condition.

Nimble Escape. The mercenary goblin can take the Disengage or Hide action as a bonus action on each of its turns.

ACTIONS

Scimitar. *Melee Weapon Attack*: +4 to hit, reach 5 ft.; One target. Hit: 5 (1d6+2) slashing damage.

EQUIPMENT

Padded armor, shield, scimitar, mercenary pack, pouch of knickknacks

MERCENARY BUGBEAR

Medium Humanoid (Goblinoid), CE

ARMOR CLASS

16 (scale mail)

HIT POINTS

27 (5d8+5)

SPEED

30 ft.

STR 15 (+2) DEX 14 (+2) CON 13 (+1) INT 08 (-1) WIS 11 (+0) CHA 09 (-1)

SKILLS Stealth +6, Survival +2

SENSES Darkvision 60 ft., passive Perception 10

LANGUAGES Goblinoid

CHALLENGE 2 (450 xp)

Brute. A melee weapon deals one extra die of its damage when the mercenary bugbear hits with it (included in the attack).

Martial Advantage. Once per turn, the mercenary bugbear can deal an extra 8 (2d6) damage to a creature it hits with a weapon attack if that creature is within 5 feet of an ally of the mercenary bugbear that isn't *incapacitated*.

ACTIONS

Glaive. *Melee Weapon Attack*: +4 to hit, reach 10 ft.; One target. Hit: 14 (2d10+2) slashing damage.

Javelin. *Melee or Ranged Weapon Attack*: +4 to hit, reach 5 feet, or range 30/120 ft.; One target. Hit: 6 (1d6+2) piercing damage.

EQUIPMENT

Scale mail, glaive, 4 javelins, mercenary pack, sac of dried meat

KOBOLD AMBUSHER

Small Humanoid (Kobold), LE

ARMOR CLASS

13 (padded armor)

HIT POINTS

8 (3d6-2)

SPEED

30 ft.

STR 07 (-2) DEX 15 (+2) CON 09 (-1) INT 08 (-1) WIS 07 (-2) CHA 08 (-1)

SKILLS Stealth +4

SENSES Darkvision 60 ft., passive Perception 08

LANGUAGES Draconic

CHALLENGE ¼ (50 xp)

Ambush. The kobold ambusher gains *advantage* on one attack against a creature who has not acted yet in the combat encounter.

Daylight Adaptability. Kobold ambushers do not suffer from sunlight sensitivity.

ACTIONS

Shortsword. *Melee Weapon Attack*: +4 to hit, reach 5 ft.; One target. Hit: 6 (1d6+2) piercing damage.

Sling. *Ranged Weapon Attack:* +4 to hit, range 30/120 ft.; One target. Hit: 5 (1d4+2) bludgeoning damage.

EQUIPMENT

Padded armor, shortsword, sling, pouch with 20 sling bullets, mercenary pack, shiny rock collection

Name: Clan Frosthammer

Nickname: Snow Troopers, Frost-beards

Symbol: Four conjoined stylized dwarven hammers in blue, often on a white background. Displayed on shields and worn on coats.

Type: Standing/Fixed

Size: Battalion; 90/20

Cost: 500 gp/240 gp/100 gp per week

Leader: Balinda Frosthammer (CG Dwarf female Sorcerer 12)

Captains: 2; *Durian Frosthammer (CG Dwarf male Fighter 11), Reginold The Ice Climber (CG Dwarf male Ranger 9)

Lieutenants: 4

Alignment: CG

Formation: The Frosthammers field 35 *heavy foot*, 25 *mercenary priests*, and 10 *mercenary sorcerers* as their primary battle formation. A unit of 20 *dire wolf riders* acts as advanced scouts and skirmishers.

Expertise: Single/Sustained Battle

Trustworthiness: 4

Base: Hall of Heroes; Darkfrost Mountains (Rusk Tribal Lands)

Sphere of Operations: Kingdom of Jutan (Merdah), Gorlan Hills, Rusk Tribal Lands

Government: Clan

Tactics: The Frosthammers use typical tactics on the battlefield. The amount of magical might they can bring to bear is considerable for a company of their size. They excel in cold weather fighting and executing maneuvers in deep snow. Because of these two things, they are often called to help rid the area of Goblinoid raiders who prey on merchant traffic through the Gorlan Hills.

    The Clan is relatively new to the planet of Shin'ar. Most inhabitants have never seen an arctic dwarf, so their appearance is still something of a novelty. Balinda Frosthammer is kind and motherly and is known to be a fair negotiator.

Logistics: The Clan is equipped with **above average** arms and armor. Smiths in the employ of the company make use of the iron deposits found around their mountaintop home and forge expertly crafted weapons and armor. Not distrustful of magic by any means, the dwarves of Clan Frosthammer have managed to acquire quite a fortune in magical items in their short time on the planet. Roughly 40% of the soldiers in the company will have a common or uncommon magic item.

History: On their home planet, Clan Frosthammer lived in a series of mountain caves they called Snowhome. Eight years ago, a freak blizzard in the middle of summer trapped almost two hundred clan members in a cavern where they were mining new veins of mithril ore found just months prior. In the middle of the night, several clan members disappeared when they fell into an open portal. An expedition was mounted at once, and several scouts were sent through the portal to find their missing clan mates.

    The scouts managed to return with news from the other side. They found the missing dwarves, who managed to escape the unknown cave they found themselves in and told the clan leaders that most of them wished to stay. Apparently, the caves in which they appeared were filled with thick iron and silver veins, more abundant than ever recorded by the Clan.

    Mining expeditions followed soon after, with provisions and building materials to create a camp for the courageous workers. The portal remained open for eight weeks, allowing hundreds of dwarves to pass through and return with carts full of ore. As mysteriously as the portal appeared, it vanished without a trace. The clan elders estimate that almost 180 dwarves were trapped on the other side.

    Dorvil Frosthammer, the leader of the mining expedition, did his best to alleviate the fears of his people as they found themselves stranded on an alien planet with no means to return. He instituted a building program that gave the clan a permanent place to live, and he began sending scouts out to neighboring communities that the clan had recently been made aware of.

    His daughter, Balinda, would go on to form the company six years later, partially to earn coin for the clan, but also to demonstrate to their neighbors the fighting prowess and tenacity of arctic dwarves.

They are now a common sight among the settlements of Northern Jutan, and they have even been named War-Brothers of the Elk tribe of Rusk, whom they initially fought against but earned their respect after a handful of hard-fought engagements with the simian tribesmen.

Notable NPCs: Dire Wolf Rider

DIRE WOLF

Large Beast, Unaligned

ARMOR CLASS
16 (natural, barding)

HIT POINTS
37 (5d10+10)

SPEED
50 ft.

STR 17 (+3) DEX 15 (+2) CON 15 (+2) INT 03 (-4) WIS 12 (+1) CHA 07 (-2)

SKILLS Perception +3, Stealth +3
SENSES passive Perception 13
LANGUAGES —
CHALLENGE 1 (200 xp)

Keen Hearing and Smell. The dire wolf has *advantage* on Wisdom (Perception) checks that rely on hearing or smell.

Pack Tactics. The dire wolf has *advantage* on an attack roll against a creature if at least one of the dire wolf's allies is within 5 feet of the creature and, the ally isn't incapacitated.

ACTIONS

Bite. *Melee Weapon Attack*: +5 to hit, reach 5 ft.; One target. Hit: 10 (2d6+3) piercing damage. If the target is a creature, it must succeed on a DC 13 Strength saving throw or be knocked *prone*.

DIRE WOLF RIDER

Medium Humanoid (Dwarf), CG

ARMOR CLASS
18 (chain mail, shield)

HIT POINTS
63 (9d8+18)

SPEED
30 ft.

STR 18 (+4) DEX 12 (+1) CON 17 (+3) INT 10 (+0) WIS 13 (+1) CHA 12 (+1)

SKILLS Animal Handling +3, Perception +3
SENSES Darkvision 60 ft., passive Perception 13
LANGUAGES Dwarvish, Tradespeech
CHALLENGE 2 (450 xp)

Charge. If the dire wolf rider moves at least 30 feet straight toward a target and then hits it with a spear attack on the same turn, the target takes an extra 10 (3d6) piercing damage.

ACTIONS

Multiattack. The dire wolf rider makes two attacks with their spear or two attacks with their shortbow.

Spear. *Melee Weapon Attack*: +6 to hit, reach 5 ft.; One target. Hit: 8 (1d6+4) piercing damage.

Shortbow. *Ranged Weapon Attack*: +3 to hit, range 80/320 ft.; One target. Hit: 5 (1d6+1) piercing damage.

EQUIPMENT

Chain mail, shield, spear, shortbow, quiver with 20 arrows, mercenary pack, military saddle, sac of dried meat snacks

Name: Company of the Damned

Nickname: Nightmare Fuel, The Circus of the Damned

Symbol: A black and gray hex with two sinister hands and two darkened celestial crowns. Flown from flags and banners but never worn.

Type: Standing/Fixed

Size: Regiment; 310/0

Cost: 350 gp/200 gp/0 gp per week

Leader: Jevera Tzeng (LE Drampyr female Wizard 15)

Captains: 1; *Yarzin Taab (LE Drampyr male Cleric 12)

Lieutenants: 2

Alignment: LE

Formation: The company forms up 160 *zombie light foot* with 100 *skeletal archers*. They are backed up and led by 35 *wraith commanders*. Jevera personally leads a unit of 15 *mercenary necromancers* into battle when magical might needs to be demonstrated.

Expertise: Guard Duty, Single/Sustained Battle

Trustworthiness: 4

Base: Darkwatch Tower; Kingdom of Eltra

Sphere of Operations: Kingdom of Eltra, Verigal (Palous), Dark Sun Woods

Government: Dictatorship

Tactics: There is little in the way of battle tactics practiced by the Company of the Damned. The undead troops lack the intelligence and foresight to interpret the instructions given to them other than to follow them to the exact word. The lack of tactics is helped by having the wraith commanders embedded with the foot soldiers to make sure every trooper is moving in the same direction.

Logistics: The company outfits their troops with **poor** arms and equipment. Often times, weapons and armor are taken off of killed soldiers and given to the next animated body that fills the ranks. To distinguish her undead soldiers from the rest of the undead that populates and roams the kingdom, Jevera clothes them in colorful motley, leading to the company being called a circus behind her back.

Jevera and her command staff have numerous magical items on them and can bring considerable magical might to any battle.

History: The company owes its allegiance to a Cabal, one of many secretive groups that seek to control the Kingdom of Eltra from the shadows. Jevera Tzeng is a senior member of the Cabal known as the Black Goats. The Black Goats control the flow of living slaves into the kingdom, and Jevera is responsible for safeguarding transports. To facilitate this, she formed the company with her lover Yarzin Taab to help not only protect the shipments but to earn coin for her personal coffers as well.

Only operating for less than a decade, the undead mercenary company has earned a reputation for never going against a contract and never fleeing from battle. The last one is easy since the soldiers have no concept of courage or fear. The nobility of the kingdom is not aware of Jevera's affiliation with a Cabal. If they did, Jevera and her commanders would have been destroyed long ago.

Notable NPCs: Zombie Light Foot, Skeletal Archer, Wraith Commander, Mercenary Necromancer

ZOMBIE LIGHT FOOT

Medium Undead, NE

ARMOR CLASS
13 (chain shirt, shield)

HIT POINTS
22 (3d8+9)

SPEED
20 ft.

STR 13 (+1) DEX 08 (-2) CON 16 (+3) INT 03 (-4) WIS 06 (-2) CHA 05 (-3)

SAVING THROWS Wisdom +0
DAMAGE IMMUNITIES Poison
CONDITION IMMUNITIES
Poisoned

SENSES Darkvision 60 ft.,passive Perception 08

LANGUAGES Understands Eltra'urk but can't speak

CHALLENGE ½ (100 xp)

Turn Resistance. The considerable power that animated the zombie foot soldier grants it a +2 bonus to resist being turned or destroyed by a cleric or paladin's turn undead ability.

Undead Fortitude. If damage reduces the zombie foot soldier to 0 hit points, it must make a Constitution saving throw with a DC of 5 + the damage taken, unless the damage is radiant or from a critical hit. On a success, the zombie foot soldier drops to 1 hit point instead.

ACTIONS

Spear. Melee Weapon Attack: +3 to hit, reach 5 ft.; One target. Hit: 5 (1d6+1) piercing damage.

Slam. Melee Weapon Attack: +3 to hit, reach 5 ft.; One target. Hit: 5 (1d6+1) bludgeoning damage.

EQUIPMENT

Rusty chain shirt, shield, spear

SKELETAL ARCHER

Medium Undead, LE

ARMOR CLASS
13 (padded)

HIT POINTS
13 (2d8+4)

SPEED
30 ft.

STR 10 (+0) DEX 14 (+2) CON 15 (+2) INT 06 (-2) WIS 08 (-1) CHA 05 (-3)

DAMAGE IMMUNITIES Poison
CONDITION IMMUNITIES
Poisoned, exhaustion

DAMAGE VULNERABILITIES
Bludgeoning

SENSES Darkvision 60 ft., passive Perception 09

LANGUAGES Understands Eltra'urk but can't speak

CHALLENGE ¼ (50 xp)

Turn Resistance. The considerable power that animated the skeletal archer grants it a +2 bonus to resist being turned or destroyed by a cleric or paladin's turn undead ability.

ACTIONS

Shortbow. Ranged Weapon Attack: +4 to hit, range 80/320 ft.; One target. Hit: 6 (1d6+2) piercing damage.

Dagger. Melee Weapon Attack: +4 to hit, reach 5 ft.; One target. Hit: 5 (1d4+2) piercing damage.

EQUIPMENT

Padded armor, dagger, shortbow, quiver with 40 arrows

WRAITH COMMANDER
Medium Undead, NE

ARMOR CLASS
13
HIT POINTS
67 (9d8+27)
SPEED
0 ft., Fly 60 ft. (Hover)

STR 06 (-2) DEX 16 (+3) CON 16 (+3) INT 12 (+1) WIS 14 (+2) CHA 15 (+2)

DAMAGE RESISTANCE Acid, cold, fire, lightning, thunder; bludgeoning, piercing, and slashing weapons from nonmagical attacks not made with silvered weapons
DAMAGE IMMUNITIES Necrotic, poison
CONDITION IMMUNITIES
Charmed, exhaustion, grappled, paralyzed, petrified, poisoned, prone, restrained
SENSES Darkvision 60 ft., passive Perception 12
LANGUAGES Eltra'urk
CHALLENGE 5 (1,800 xp)

Incorporeal Movement. The wraith commander can move through other creatures and objects as if they were difficult terrain. It takes 5 (1d10) force damage if it ends its turn inside an object.

Turn Resistance. The considerable power that animated the wraith commander grants it a +2 bonus to resist being turned or destroyed by a cleric or paladin's turn undead ability.

Sunlight Sensitivity. While in sunlight, the wraith has *disadvantage* on attack rolls, as well on Wisdom (Perception) checks that rely on sight.

Suppressed Ability. Through necrotic manipulation, the wraith commander's create specter ability is suppressed. This is to ensure the wraith commander does not become uncontrollable as it amasses specter minions.

ACTIONS

Life Drain. Melee Weapon Attack: +6 to hit, reach 5 ft.; One creature. Hit: 21 (4d8+3) necrotic damage. The target must succeed on a DC 14 Constitution saving throw or its hit point maximum is reduced by an amount equal to the damage taken. This reduction lasts until the target finishes a long rest. The target dies if this effect reduces its hit point maxim to 0.

MERCENARY NECROMANCER
Medium Humanoid (Drampyr), LE

ARMOR CLASS
12 (*robe of protection*)
HIT POINTS
49 (9d8+9)
SPEED
30 ft.

STR 10 (+0) DEX 12 (+1) CON 12 (+1) INT 18 (+4) WIS 14 (+2) CHA 11 (+0)

SKILLS Arcana +6, Insight +4
SENSES Darkvision 60 ft., passive Perception 12
LANGUAGES Eltra'urk, Infernal, Tradespeech
CHALLENGE 6 (2,300 xp)

Spellcasting. The mercenary necromancer is a level 9 spellcaster (DC 14, +6 spell attack).

Cantrips (at will): blade ward, chill touch, mage hand, shocking grasp

Level 1 (4 slots): false life, magic missile, ray of sickness

Level 2 (3 slots): darkness, hold person

Level 3 (3 slots): animate dead, stinking cloud

Level 4 (3 slots): evard's black tentacles

Level 5 (1 slot): cloud kill

Unholy Animation. Undead beings the mercenary necromancer animates gain a +2 bonus to resist being turned or destroyed.

ACTIONS

Dagger. Melee Weapon Attack: +3 to hit, reach 5 ft.; One target. Hit: 4 (1d4+1) piercing damage.

EQUIPMENT

Robe of protection, dagger, arcane focus or spell component pouch, mercenary pack

Name: Company of the Fang

Nickname: Beast Men

Symbol: A set of fangs on a white and red field. Worn on clothing and flown on flags.

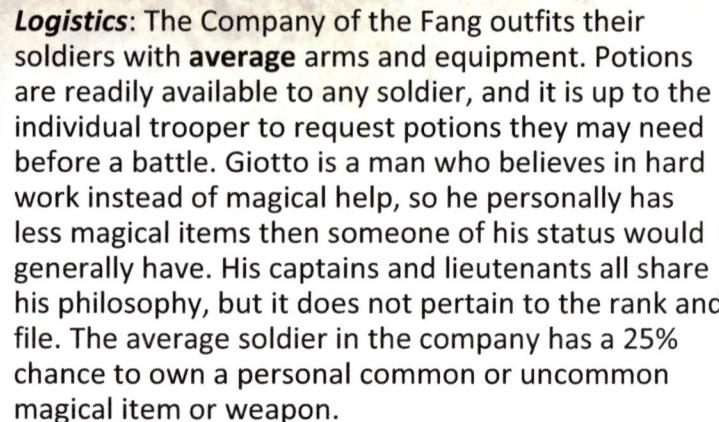

Type: Standing/Fixed

Size: Brigade; 150/25

Cost: 400 gp/220 gp/75 gp per week

Leader: Giotto Mele de Laark (N Werebear male Ranger 12)

Captains: 3; *Simon Octavio de Laark (N Werestag male Druid 11), Arturo Thicktusk (CN Wereboar male Barbarian 8), Jovanna Relargo de Laark (NE Wererat female Rogue 7)

Lieutenants: 3

Alignment: N

Formation: The company forms up 50 *werebear vanguard* backed by 45 *wererat skirmishers*. A force of 30 *wereboar berserkers* and 10 *werewolf ambushers* roam the battlefield disrupting enemy positions. A small unit of 15 *werestag druids* hangs back from the front line, ready to receive and heal wounded soldiers.

Expertise: Single/Sustained Battle

Trustworthiness: 3

Base: The town of Laark; Dark Sun Woods

Sphere of Operations: Dark Sun Woods, Verigal (Palous, Northsea)

Government: Council

Tactics: The Company of the Fang seems disorganized to other companies. Their inherent savagery is apparent as soon as they form ranks, which are always loose and full of gaps. This is more by design then hap stance. The apparent disorganization has often lead to their enemies underestimating them. Once the battle is joined, the soldiers of the Company of the Fang display brilliant maneuvers that take advantage of their supernatural quickness and strengths.

Giotto personally negotiates contracts. He is known to be fair; however, he can also be aloof and unmoving when it comes to deals that have his company despoil the wilderness in some way. He rarely sends away potential employers, but he is known to change the agreements mid-battle for conditions that are more favorable to him and his people.

Logistics: The Company of the Fang outfits their soldiers with **average** arms and equipment. Potions are readily available to any soldier, and it is up to the individual trooper to request potions they may need before a battle. Giotto is a man who believes in hard work instead of magical help, so he personally has less magical items then someone of his status would generally have. His captains and lieutenants all share his philosophy, but it does not pertain to the rank and file. The average soldier in the company has a 25% chance to own a personal common or uncommon magical item or weapon.

History: Centuries ago, the people of the town of Cassca were cursed by a powerful woods witch. The curse was further empowered by a rising spike in mana, and the massive accumulation of magical power warped the curse to include not just the townsfolk, but their offspring for several generations after. The curse transformed all of the townsfolk into all manor of Lycanthropes. This horrific act caused many of them to lose their minds. Some attacked their neighbors; others ran off into the woods, never to be seen again. Enough of them kept a shred of sanity to come to the conclusion that they were a danger to everyone, so the town was abandoned as the transformed townsfolk melted into the southern Dark Sun Woods to live the rest of their lives as beast-men. Over several generations, the cursed beings forgot what it was like to be human and even forgot how to transform back into a human being. They lived as beasts, roaming the forest in tribes that often warred with each other for resources and territory.

Centuries later, the newest generation of Lycans who were decedents of the originally cursed townsfolk began to revert back to their human form. They began to move from their caves and treetop homes to the forest floor, and once enough of them had regained their humanity, they set about building a new town for their new lives. Giotto is the grandson of one of the first founders of the town of Laark, the haven for the Dark Sun Lycans. He got together like-minded individuals and brought them south out of the woods to ply their trade among their former Vergal countrymen.

Notable NPCs: Werebear Vanguard, Wererat Skirmishers, Wereboar Berserker, Werewolf Ambusher, Werestag Druid

Special Note: Lycans who hail from the town of Laark never go about in their human form unless they are attempting to hide their nature. To them, their hybrid form is their true form.

WEREBEAR VANGUARD

Medium Lycanthrope (Werebear), N

ARMOR CLASS
16 (breastplate, shield)

HIT POINTS
135 (18d8+54)

SPEED
40 ft., Climb 30 ft.

STR 19 (+4) DEX 10 (+0) CON 17 (+3) INT 11 (+0) WIS 12 (+1) CHA 12 (+1)

SKILLS Perception +7, Survival +3

DAMAGE IMMUNITIES
Bludgeoning, piercing, and slashing from nonmagical attacks not made with silvered weapons

SENSES passive Perception 17

LANGUAGES Veri'urk, Tradespeech

CHALLENGE 5 (1,800 xp)

Brute. A melee weapon deals one extra die of its damage when the werebear vanguard hits with it (included in the attack).

Keen Smell. The werebear vanguard has *advantage* on Wisdom (Perception) checks that rely on smell.

Shapechanger. The werebear vanguard can use its action to polymorph into a Large bear or back to its hybrid form. Any equipment it is wearing or carrying isn't transformed. It reverts to human form if it dies.

ACTIONS

Multiattack. The werebear vanguard makes two melee attacks.

Bite. *Melee Weapon Attack*: +7 to hit, reach 5 ft.; One target. Hit: 15 (2d10+4) piercing damage. If the target is humanoid, it must succeed on a DC 14 Constitution saving throw or be cursed with werebear lycanthropy.

Claw. *Melee Weapon Attack*: +7 to hit, reach 5 ft.; One target. Hit: 13 (2d8+4) slashing damage.

Battleaxe. *Melee Weapon Attack*: +7 to hit, reach 5 ft.; One target. Hit: 13 (2d8+4) slashing damage.

EQUIPMENT
Breastplate, battleaxe, mercenary pack, shield

WERERAT SKIRMISHER

Medium Lycanthrope (Wererat), NE

ARMOR CLASS
13 (leather)

HIT POINTS
33 (6d8+6)

SPEED
30 ft.

STR 10(+0) DEX 15 (+2) CON 12 (+1) INT 11 (+0) WIS 10 (+0) CHA 08 (-1)

SKILLS Perception +2, Stealth +4

DAMAGE IMMUNITIES
Bludgeoning, piercing, and slashing from nonmagical attacks not made with silvered weapons

SENSES passive Perception 12

LANGUAGES Veri'urk, Tradespeech

CHALLENGE 3 (700 xp)

Keen Smell. The wererat skirmisher has *advantage* on Wisdom (Perception) checks that rely on smell.

Shapechanger. The wererat skirmisher can use its action to polymorph into a giant rat or back to its hybrid form. Any equipment it is wearing or carrying isn't transformed. It reverts to human form if it dies.

Sneak Attack. Once per turn, the wererat skirmisher deals an extra 7 (2d6) damage when it hits a target with a weapon attack and has *advantage* on the attack roll, or when the target is within 5 feet of an ally of the wererat skirmisher that isn't *incapacitated* and the wererat skirmisher does not have *disadvantage* on the attack roll.

ACTIONS

Multiattack. The wererat skirmisher can make one bite, and one mace attack or two ranged weapon attacks.

Bite. *Melee Weapon Attack*: +4 to hit, reach 5 ft.; One target. Hit: 4 (1d4+2) piercing damage. If the target is a humanoid, it must succeed on a DC 11 Constitution saving throw or be cursed with wererat lycanthropy.

Mace. Melee Weapon Attack: +2 to hit, reach 5 ft.; One target. Hit: 4 (1d6) bludgeoning damage.

Shortbow. Ranged Weapon Attack: +4 to hit, range 80/320 ft.; One target. Hit: 7 (1d8+2) piercing damage.

EQUIPMENT

Leather armor, mace, shortbow, quiver with 30 arrows, mercenary pack

WEREBOAR BERSERKER

Medium Lycanthrope (Wereboar), CN

ARMOR CLASS
12 (hide armor)

HIT POINTS
78 (12d8+24)

SPEED
30 ft.

STR 17 (+3) DEX 10 (+0) CON 15 (+2) INT 10 (+0) WIS 11 (+0) CHA 08 (-1)

SKILLS Perception +2

DAMAGE IMMUNITIES
Bludgeoning, piercing, and slashing from nonmagical attacks not made with silvered weapons

SENSES passive Perception 12

LANGUAGES Veri'urk, Tradespeech

CHALLENGE 5 (1,800 xp)

Charge. If the wereboar berserker moves at least 15 feet straight towards a target and then hits it with its tusks on the same turn, the target takes an extra 7 (2d6) slashing damage. If the target is a creature, it must succeed on a DC 13 Strength saving throw or be knocked *prone*.

Reckless. At the start of its turn, the wereboar berserker can gain *advantage* on all melee weapon attack rolls during that turn, but attack rolls against it have *advantage* until the start of its next turn.

Relentless (Recharges after a short or long rest). If the wereboar berserker takes 14 damage or less that would reduce it to 0 hit points, it is reduced to 1 hit point instead.

Shapechanger. The wereboar berserker can use its action to polymorph into a boar or back to its hybrid form. Any equipment it is wearing or carrying isn't transformed. It reverts to human form if it dies.

ACTIONS

Multiattack. The wereboar berserker makes two melee attacks, one of which can be with its tusks.

Tusks. Melee Weapon Attack: +5 to hit, reach 5 ft.; One target. Hit: 10 (2d6+3) slashing damage. If the target is a humanoid, it must succeed on a DC 12 Constitution saving throw or be cursed with wereboar lycanthropy.

Greataxe. Melee Weapon Attack: +5 to hit, reach 10 ft.; One target. Hit: 10 (1d12+3) slashing damage.

EQUIPMENT

Hide armor, greataxe, mercenary pack

WEREWOLF AMBUSHER

Medium Lycanthrope (Werewolf), CE

ARMOR CLASS
13 (studded leather)

HIT POINTS
58 (9d8+18)

SPEED
30 ft.

STR 15 (+2) DEX 13 (+1) CON 14 (+2) INT 10 (+0) WIS 11 (+0) CHA 10 (+0)

SKILLS Perception +4, Stealth +3

DAMAGE IMMUNITIES
Bludgeoning, piercing, and slashing from nonmagical attacks not made with silvered weapons

SENSES passive Perception 14

LANGUAGES Veri'urk, Tradespeech

CHALLENGE 3 (700 xp)

Ambusher. The werewolf ambusher gains *advantage* on melee attacks against a creature who has not had its turn in combat yet.

Keen Hearing and Smell. The werewolf ambusher gains *advantage* on Wisdom (Perception) checks that rely on hearing or smell.

Shapechanger. The werewolf ambusher can use its action to polymorph into a wolf or back to its hybrid form. Any equipment it is wearing or carrying isn't transformed. It reverts to human form if it dies.

ACTIONS

Multiattack. The werewolf ambusher makes two melee attacks: one with its bite and one with its claws or spear.

Bite. *Melee Weapon Attack*: +4 to hit, reach 5 ft.; One target. Hit: 6 (1d8+2) piercing damage. If the target is a humanoid, it must succeed on a DC 12 Constitution saving throw or be cursed with werewolf lycanthropy.

Claws. *Melee Weapon Attack*: +4 to hit, reach 5 ft.; One target. Hit: 7 (2d4+2) slashing damage.

Spear. *Melee or Ranged Weapon Attack*: +4 to hit, reach 5 feet, or range 20/60 ft.; One target. Hit: 5 (1d6+2) piercing damage or 6 (1d8+2) piercing damage if used with two hands to make a melee attack.

EQUIPMENT

Studded leather armor, spear, mercenary pack

WERESTAG DRUID

Medium Lycanthrope (Werestag), N

ARMOR CLASS
12 (unarmored)
HIT POINTS
33 (6d8+6)
SPEED
30 ft.

STR 10 (+0)	DEX 15 (+2)	CON 12 (+1)	INT 11 (+0)	WIS 14 (+2)	CHA 12 (+1)

SKILLS Perception +4, Nature +4
DAMAGE IMMUNITIES
Bludgeoning, piercing, and slashing from nonmagical attacks not made with silvered weapons
SENSES passive Perception 14
LANGUAGES Veri'urk, Tradespeech
CHALLENGE 3 (700 xp)

Keen Smell. The werestag druid gains *advantage* on Wisdom (Perception) checks that rely on smell.

Shapechanger. The werestag druid can use its action to polymorph into a deer or back to its hybrid form. Any equipment it is wearing or carrying isn't transformed. It reverts to human form if it dies.

Spellcasting. The werestag druid is a level 6 spellcaster (DC 13, +5 spell attacks).

Cantrips (at will): *druidcraft, resistance, thorn whip*

Level 1 (4 slots): *create or destroy water, cure wounds, entangle, healing word*

Level 2 (3 slots): *barkskin, gust of wind, spike growth*

Level 3 (2 slots): *dispel magic, sleet storm*

ACTIONS

Multiattack. The werestag druid makes two melee attacks, only one of which can be a bite.

Bite. *Melee Weapon Attack*: +5 to hit, reach 5 ft.; One target. Hit: 5 (1d4+2) piercing damage. If the target is a humanoid, it must succeed on a DC 11 Constitution saving throw or be cursed with werestag lycanthropy.

Antlers. *Melee Weapon Attack*: +3 to hit, reach 5 ft.; One target. Hit: 3 (1d4) piercing damage.

Quarterstaff. *Melee Weapon Attack*: +3 to hit, reach 5 ft.; One target. Hit: 4 (1d6) bludgeoning damage or 5 (1d8) bludgeoning damage if used with two hands.

EQUIPMENT

Quarterstaff, druidic focus, herbalism kit, mercenary pack

Name: Crimson Daggers

Nickname: Red Blades

Symbol: A crimson knife (dagger) on a white field. Never flown or worn on clothing. Members of the company get the symbol tattooed on their arm or chest.

Type: Standing/Fixed

Size: Troop; 60/0

Cost: 800 gp/270 gp/0 gp per week

Leader: Feronia Caal (NE Vampyr female Rogue 12)

Captains: 1; *Galvin Raab (NE Vampyr male Sorcerer 9)

Lieutenants: 2

Alignment: NE

Formation: The Crimson Daggers consist of 35 *mercenary ambushers*, 20 *mercenary archers*, and 5 *mercenary sorcerers*.

Expertise: Single/Sustained Battle

Trustworthiness: 3

Base: The Crimson Loft (manor house); Marisco (Verigal)

Sphere of Operations: Verigal (Northsea, Esta, Sylvar)

Government: Dictatorship

Tactics: The Crimson Daggers form units that consist of anywhere from eight to eleven soldiers. These units are spaced out and often act autonomously from their counterparts. Ambushes and sneak attacks are the favored tactics, severely thinning their opposition in the process.

Feronia lets Galvin negotiate contracts, and he acts as the face of the company. The less Feronia has to deal with the general public, the better in her book.

Logistics: The company is equipped with **above average** arms and armor. Feronia believes in rewarding her troops with magic as well as coin, so almost 40% of her soldiers will have a personal common or uncommon magical item.

History: Feronia was born in Eltra to a down-and-out street musician who found herself the object of desire for a vampire noble. A year-long romance led to the birth of Feronia, and she and her mother subsequently dumped back on the street when her father grew bored with them.

Her mother died just after her fourth birthday, leaving Feronia alone on the streets. Like many youths in her position, she was scooped up by a gang of ruffians who protected her and taught her the ways of the street. She spent twelve years in the gang, learning how to pickpockets and break into secure residences. A coup led to her leaving the gang before she was killed, and she traveled out of Eltra altogether with a small group of friends. Galvin Raab was one of those companions, and the two of them grew very close. They both joined a number of adventuring parties that traveled the planet before returning to Eltra and Verigal where they pooled their coin and formed the Crimson Daggers.

Name: Drunken Bandits

Nickname: Traveling Tavern Brawl, The Broken Chair Leg Society of Reformed Killers

Symbol: A foaming mug on a white field. Flow on flags and displayed on shields.

Type: Standing/Fixed

Size: Battalion; 95/20

Cost: 400 gp/180 gp/45 gp per week

Leader: Ivor Torfson (CN Human male Rogue 8/Bard 6)

Captains: 2; *Brunhilde Ivordottor (CN Half-elf female Bard 7), Havord The Red Faced (CN Human male Barbarian 4/Bard 3)

Lieutenants: 2

Alignment: N

Formation: The Drunken Bandits field 35 *heavy foot*, 10 *mercenary acolytes*, and 20 *mercenary archers* as their main attacking force. They are supplemented with 20 *mercenary berserkers* and a unit of 10 *skald skirmishers*.

Expertise: Single/Sustained Battle, War

Trustworthiness: 4

Base: The Hall (fortified manor); Kingdom of Jutan (Clawbite Hills)

Sphere of Operations: Kingdom of Jutan (Clawbite Hills), Jutal Forest, Empire of Alteria (Northern Hinterlands)

Government: Brotherhood

Tactics: The Drunken Bandits are truly a sight to see on the battlefield.

Seemingly undisciplined and unruly, the company forms loose lines until commanded to tighten up. Once a battle is joined, they fight with precision and prowess one would expect from professional soldiers. Off the battlefield, the troopers can be found drinking away their aches and pains in one of the company's mobile taverns, which in reality is little more than a large tent with several tapped kegs and cheaply crafted furniture.

Contracts come often to the company, despite their reputation as being loud and undisciplined. Ivor and his daughter treat every soldier as a member of their family. The benefit of the doubt is given often, and minor infractions are handled with simple manual labor punishments. However, more severe discipline is swift and brutal to those who routinely break the rules or whose antics damage the reputation of the company.

Logistics: The company is outfitted with **average** arms and armor. A lot of the coin gained from contracts goes to keeping the soldiers fed and swimming in ale. Simple potions, such as *potions of healing*, are given to each soldier, and they can request replacement potions anytime. Roughly 20% of the company, not including captains and lieutenants, will have a personal common or uncommon magical item as well.

History: Twenty-eight years ago, Ivor Torfson joined a group of bandits who waylaid caravans headed south from the Jarland of the Southern Shore. Coin came quickly and often, prompting the bandits to go after larger fair. A daring attack on a small castle would be the group's downfall as the castle was protected by a powerful individual who recently found themselves marooned on the planet. She was known as The Azure Specter, but in reality she was an elven archmage who found herself in need of assistance after she understood that getting back to her own planet was next to impossible. She entered into an agreement with the small noble family who owned the castle; in exchange for her protection, they would supply her with a place to live and a lab in which to continue her experiments on the Manasphere.

The bandit's attack was folly from the very beginning. After letting them quietly sneak over the castle's walls, they were then singled out and either struck immobile by her trap spells or blasted to ash by her powerful wards. Ivor was among the few survivors, who were then imprisoned in the castle's dungeon.

Local law gave permission for the noble family to hold their prisoners indefinitely, though most of the surviving bandits were let go after serving two years in irons. Some were executed when it came to light that they had harmed or killed in their career as a bandit. Ivor found himself deeply enamored with the archmage who was his jailor, and in turn, she began to develop feelings for him. When he was released, he asked to stay, and the two were quickly wed. The romance lasted only a short while. After giving birth to a daughter, the archmage made a breakthrough that allowed her to safely open a portal to her native planet. Sad, but completely understanding of her intent to return to her home, Ivor said goodbye to his love as she disappeared into a portal of her own conjuring.

Unsure what to do with himself and how to earn coin, Ivor returned to the only life he understood: banditry. After giving his young daughter to an elderly couple to look after, Ivor traveled the kingdom joining bandit groups here and there, earning just enough coin to live. A realization struck him; what if he could entice his fellow bandits into using their skill sets to earn coin without breaking the law. After a year of "going straight," his group of reformed bandits had earned more gold fighting professionally then they had ever earned robbing people. As their reputation grew, the contracts came with increased frequency, and Ivor made enough gold to build himself a home. He sent for his daughter and raised her with the help of his fellow soldiers. She grew up surrounded by drunken killers, but good-natured killers at that. She is poised to take over leadership of the company from her father, and each and every soldier will gladly lay down their life for her.

Notable NPCs: Skald Skirmisher

Special Note: All Drunken Bandit soldiers, lieutenants, and captains gain the <u>Tavern Brawler</u> feat for free.

SKALD SKIRMISHER

Medium Humanoid (Human), CN

ARMOR CLASS
15 (chain shirt)

HIT POINTS
28 (4d8+4)

SPEED
30 ft.

STR 12 (+1) DEX 14 (+2) CON 12 (+1) INT 13 (+1) WIS 11 (+0) CHA 16 (+3)

SKILLS Acrobatics +4, Perception +2, Performance +5

SENSES passive Perception 12

LANGUAGES Juten, Tradespeech

CHALLENGE 1 (200 xp)

Inspiration. The skald skirmisher can grant a d6 to an ally for them to use and add the number to a single ability check, attack roll, or saving throw. They can grant inspiration three times before needing a long rest.

Spellcasting. The skald skirmisher is a level 4 spellcaster (DC 13, +5 to spell attacks).

Cantrips (at will): blade ward, minor illusion, vicious mockery

Level 1 (4 slots): bane, cure wounds, tasha's hideous laughter

Level 2 (2 slots): hold person, silence

ACTIONS

Rapier. Melee Weapon Attack: +4 to hit, reach 5 ft.; One target. Hit: 7 (1d8+2) piercing damage.

Light Crossbow. Ranged Weapon Attack: +4 to hit, range 80/320 ft.; One target. Hit: 7 (1d8+2) piercing damage.

EQUIPMENT

Chain shirt, rapier, light crossbow, crossbow bolt case with 20 crossbow bolts, mercenary pack, musical instrument

---

Name: The Darktide

Nickname: The Death Dealers, The Dark Horde

Symbol: The Drow symbol for "war won through might" depicted on a black or white field. Worn on clothing and armor but never flown on flags or banners.

Type: Standing/Fixed

Size: Brigade; 170/20

Cost: 380 gp/175 gp/70 gp per week

Leader: Xander Xol'aster (NE Drow male Wizard 14)

Captains: 1; *Xavin Xol'aster (NE Drow male Fighter 14)

Lieutenants: 2

Alignment: NE

Formation: A formidable group of 100 *goblin irregulars*, 20 *troll skirmishers*, 25 *bugbear marauders*, and 5 *ettin vanguard* makes up the company's main attacking force. A unit comprising of 15 *drow elite ambushers* and 5 *drow warrior mages* roam the battlefield intent on ending any opposition quickly.

Expertise: Single/Sustained Battle

Trustworthiness: 3

Base: Sel'delmah (underground); Bronze Mountains (Northern Tip)

Sphere of Operations: Northern Tip, Rusk Tribal Lands

Government: Dictatorship

Tactics: The tactics used by the Darktide are best summed up as "organized chaos." The attacking force lines up the best a group of dim-witted battle fodder can muster, and they are more-or-less pointed at an enemy and let loose. Opponents that display more than a rudimentary level of warcraft are first whittled down by the drow members of the company.

Xander and his brother negotiate all contracts personally. They ensure they get top coin for their services, and they use their riches to make sure their small community remains self-sufficient, and most of all, secret from the prying eyes of the white dragon siblings that rule the forest above their home.

Logistics: The average soldier in the company is equipped with **poor** arms and armor. The Drow members are given **superb** weapons and equipment. Magical items are scarce among the non-Drow but almost all of the Drow troops will have a personal uncommon or rare magical item or weapon, including potions and wands.

History: Like many racial groups, the Drow masters of the Darktide are not native to the planet of Shin'ar. Many centuries ago, a group of powerful Drow managed to find the planet and began to experiment with the abundance of magical energy found in the atmosphere. The most powerful of them managed to imprison a demon and used its power to fuel their magical experiments. Eventually, the demon would be released by the double-dealings of a trio of white dragon siblings that fled their territory and encountered the secretive Drow. The demon went on to slaughter most of the elves. Only a small handful managed to escape further underground.

Time passed, and the survivors did the best they could to live and thrive on the alien planet. Years later, during a turbulent time known as a Lunar Quickening, the Drow managed to open a portal to their native realm and entice almost 80 more houseless rogues and non-noble females to join them on Shin'ar. They formed a small village deep underground they named Sel'delmah, a Drow word loosely translated to "New Home."

Now, with enough power and might to affect their circumstances, the Drow went on to conquer a number of Goblinoid tribes that laired near their new home. Most of them were turned into slaves, but just enough were outfitted with weapons and armor and turned into a reasonably successful mercenary company that plied their trade to anyone who could afford their price. The Drow are especially careful not to attract too much attention to themselves, as the memories of the dragons who slaughtered their brethren are long, and their claws are sharp. The dragons are sure to attempt to finish them off before the dark elves become too powerful to reckon with.

Notable NPCs: Goblin Irregular, Troll Skirmisher, Bugbear Marauder, Ettin Vanguard, Drow Elite Ambusher, Drow Warrior Mage

GOBLIN IRREGULAR
Small Humanoid (Goblin), NE

ARMOR CLASS
13 (leather armor)

HIT POINTS
7 (2d6)

SPEED
30 ft.

STR 08 (-1)	DEX 14 (+2)	CON 10 (+0)	INT 10 (+0)	WIS 08 (-1)	CHA 08 (-1)

SKILLS Stealth +6
SENSES Darkvision 60 ft., passive Perception 09
LANGUAGES Goblinoid, Drow
CHALLENGE ¼ (50 xp)

Gang Up. The goblin irregular has *advantage* on attack rolls against a creature if at least one of the goblin irregular's allies is within 5 feet of the creature, and the ally isn't incapacitated.

ACTIONS

Shortsword. Melee Weapon Attack: +4 to hit, reach 5 ft.; One target. Hit: 6 (1d6+2) piercing damage.
Sling. Ranged Weapon Attack: +4 to hit, range 30/120 ft.; One target. Hit: 5 (1d4+2) bludgeoning damage.

EQUIPMENT

Leather armor, shortsword, sling, pouch with 20 sling bullets, mercenary pack

TROLL SKIRMISHER

Large Giant, CE

ARMOR CLASS
15 (natural)

HIT POINTS
84 (8d10+40)

SPEED
30 ft.

STR 18 (+4) DEX 13 (+1) CON 20 (+5) INT 07 (-2) WIS 09 (-1) CHA 07 (-2)

SKILLS Perception +2

SENSES Darkvision 60 ft., passive Perception 12

LANGUAGES Giant

CHALLENGE 6 (2,300 xp)

Blood Frenzy. Troll skirmishers gain *advantage* on melee attack rolls against any creature that does not have all of its hit points.

Keen Smell. The troll skirmisher has *advantage* on Wisdom (Perception) checks that rely on smell.

Regeneration. The troll skirmisher regains 10 hit points at the start of its turn. If the troll skirmisher takes acid or fire damage, this trait doesn't function at the start of the troll skirmisher's next turn. The troll skirmisher dies only if it starts its turn with 0 hit points and doesn't regenerate.

ACTIONS

Multiattack. The troll skirmisher makes three attacks: one with its bite and two with its claws.

Bite. *Melee Weapon Attack*: +7 to hit, reach 5 ft.; One target. Hit: 7 (1d6+4) piercing damage.

Claw. *Melee Weapon Attack*: +7 to hit, reach 5 ft.; One target. Hit: 11 (2d6+4) slashing damage.

EQUIPMENT
Mercenary pack

BUGBEAR MARAUDER

Medium Humanoid (Bugbear), CE

ARMOR CLASS
14 (hide armor)

HIT POINTS
27 (5d8+5)

SPEED
30 ft.

STR 15 (+2) DEX 14 (+2) CON 13 (+1) INT 08 (-1) WIS 11 (+0) CHA 09 (-1)

SKILLS Stealth +6, Survival +2

SENSES Darkvision 60 ft., passive Perception 10

LANGUAGES Goblinoid, Drow

CHALLENGE 1 (200 xp)

Brute. A melee weapon deals one extra die of its damage when the bugbear marauder hits with it (included in the attack).

Reckless. At the start of its turn, the bugbear marauder can gain *advantage* on all melee weapon attack rolls during that turn, but attack rolls against it have *advantage* until the start of its next turn.

ACTIONS

Morningstar. Melee Weapon Attack: +4 to hit, reach 5 ft.; One target. Hit: 11 (2d8+2) piercing damage.

EQUIPMENT
Hide armor, morningstar, mercenary pack

ETTIN VANGUARD

Large Giant, CE

ARMOR CLASS
14 (ring mail)

HIT POINTS
85 (10d10+30)

SPEED
40 ft.

STR 21 (+5) DEX 08 (-1) CON 17 (+3) INT 06 (-2) WIS 10 (+0) CHA 08 (-1)

SKILLS Perception +4

SENSES Darkvision 60 ft., passive Perception 14

LANGUAGES Giant, Drow

CHALLENGE 5 (1,800 xp)

Killing Frenzy. Whenever an ettin vanguard brings a creature to 0 hit points with a melee weapon attack, it gains *advantage* on its next attack roll.

Two Heads. The ettin vanguard has *advantage* on Wisdom (Perception) checks and on saving throws against being *blinded*, *charmed*, *deafened*, *frightened*, *stunned*, and *knocked unconscious*.

Wakeful. When one of the ettin vanguard's heads is asleep, its other head is awake.

ACTIONS

Multiattack. The ettin vanguard makes two attacks: one with its war pick and one with its flail.

War Pick. *Melee Weapon Attack*: +7 to hit, reach 5 ft.; One target. Hit: 14 (2d8+5) piercing damage.

Flail. *Melee Weapon Attack*: +7 to hit, reach 5 ft.; One target. Hit: 14 (2d8+5) bludgeoning damage.

EQUIPMENT

Ring mail, war pick, flail, mercenary pack

DROW ELITE AMBUSHER

Medium Humanoid (Drow), NE

ARMOR CLASS
18 (chain shirt +1)

HIT POINTS
71 (11d8+22)

SPEED
30 ft.

STR 13 (+1) DEX 18 (+4) CON 14 (+2) INT 11 (+0) WIS 13 (+1) CHA 12 (+1)

SAVING THROWS Dexterity +7, Constitution +5, Wisdom +4

DAMAGE IMMUNITY Poison

SKILLS Perception +4, Stealth +10

SENSES Darkvision 120 ft., passive Perception 14

LANGUAGES Drow, Undercommon

CHALLENGE 6 (2,300 xp)

Deadly Ambusher. The drow elite ambusher gains *advantage* on attack rolls against creatures who have not taken their turn in combat yet. In addition, they treat every successful strike against a creature who has not taken their turn yet as a critical strike.

Fey Ancestry. The drow elite ambusher has *advantage* on saving throws against being charmed, and magic can't put them to sleep.

Innate Spellcasting. The drow elite ambusher's spellcasting ability is Charisma (DC 12). It can innately cast the following spells requiring no material components:

At will: *dancing lights*

1/day each: *darkness, faerie fire, levitate (self only)*

Sunlight Sensitivity. While in sunlight, the drow elite ambusher has *disadvantage* on attack rolls, as well as on Wisdom (Perception) checks that rely on sight.

ACTIONS

Multiattack. The drow elite ambusher makes two shortbow attacks or two shortsword attacks.

Shortsword +1. Melee Weapon Attack: +8 to hit, reach 5 ft.; One target. Hit: 9 (1d6+5) piercing damage plus 10 (3d6) poison damage.

Shortbow +1. *Ranged Weapon Attack*: +8 to hit, range 80/320 ft.; One target. Hit: 9 (1d6+5) piercing damage, and the target must succeed on a DC 13 Constitution saving throw or be poisoned for 1 hour. If the saving throw fails by 5 or more points, the target is also unconscious while poisoned in this way. The target wakes up if it takes damage or if another creature takes an action to shake it awake.

EQUIPMENT

Chain shirt +1, shortsword +1, shortbow +1, quiver with 30 arrows, mercenary pack, *potion of greater healing, cloak of elvinkind*

DROW WARRIOR MAGE

Medium Humanoid (Drow), NE

ARMOR CLASS

20 (*scale mail +1, shield +1*)

HIT POINTS

65 (10d8+22)

SPEED

30 ft.

STR 13 (+1) DEX 17 (+3) CON 14 (+2) INT 17 (+3) WIS 14 (+2) CHA 13 (+1)

SAVING THROWS Dexterity +3, Constitution +3, Charisma +3

SKILLS Arcana +6, Acrobatics +6, Perception +4, Stealth +6

SENSES Darkvision 120 ft., passive Perception 14

LANGUAGES Drow, Undercommon

CHALLENGE 6 (2,300 xp)

Action Surge. The drow warrior mage can take one additional action on top of its regular action and a possible bonus action on their turn. They can do this once before a short or long rest.

Fey Ancestry. The drow warrior mage has advantage on saving throws against being charmed, and magic can't put them to sleep.

Innate Spellcasting. The drow elite ambusher's spellcasting ability is Charisma (DC 13). It can innately cast the following spells requiring no material components:

At will: dancing lights

1/day each: darkness, faerie fire, levitate (self only)

Spellcasting. The drow warrior mage is a level 8 spellcaster (DC 14, +6 spell attack).

Cantrips (at will): mage hand, minor illusion, poison spray, ray of frost

Level 1 (4 slots): magic missile, shield, witch bolt, thunderwave

Level 2 (3 slots): alter self, misty step, web

Level 3 (3 slots): lightning bolt, haste

Level 4 (2 slots): greater invisibility, wall of fire

Sunlight Sensitivity. While in sunlight, the drow elite ambusher has *disadvantage* on attack rolls, as well as on Wisdom (Perception) checks that rely on sight.

ACTIONS

Multiattack. The drow warrior mage makes two shortsword attacks.

Shortsword +1. *Melee Weapon Attack*: +7 to hit, reach 5 ft.; One target. Hit: 8 (1d6+4) piercing damage plus 10 (3d6) poison damage.

EQUIPMENT

Scale mail +1, shield +1, shortsword +1, mercenary pack, *potion of greater healing, cloak of elvenkind*, arcane focus (gem in the hilt of shortsword), *wand of gooey restraint*

NEW MAGICAL ITEM

Wand of Gooey Restraint

Wand, rare (requires attunement by a spellcaster)

This wand has 3 charges. While holding it, you can use an action to expend 1 of its charges, and a gooey glob of sticky glue shoots forth up to 30 feet, sticking to a target if it fails a DC 14 Dexterity saving throw. Stuck targets are considered *restrained* for 2 +1d6 rounds. At the end of the duration, the target is no longer *restrained*, but their movement speed is reduced by ½ for the next 10 minutes. The wand regains 1d3 charges every day at dawn. The glue cannot be dispelled, but the use of *universal solvent* dissolves the glue virtuously instantaneously.

Name: Snow Vipers

Nickname: Cold Blooded Killers, Slithering Scum

Symbol: A viper, facing sinister, on a white field. Never worn or displayed on equipment. Soldiers get the symbol tattooed somewhere visible, like the face or hands.

Type: Recruiting/Fixed

Size: Battalion; 25 (60)/10

Cost: 300 gp/190 gp/45 gp per week

Leader: Rallo Coldtounge (CE Human male Barbarian 8/Sorcerer 6)

Captains: 1; *Astiir (CE Human female Rogue 11)

Lieutenants: 2

Alignment: CE

Formation: The Snow Vipers field 40 *mercenary berserkers* with 15 *mercenary acolytes* and 10 *mercenary sorcerers*. A new unit comprised of 20 *lizardfolk mercenaries* roams the battle lines looking for opportunity.

Expertise: Single/Sustained Battle

Trustworthiness: 2

Base: Village of Winterburg; Lake of Ice

Sphere of Operations: Lake of Ice, Kingdom of Jutan (Riverfields, Merdah)

Government: Dictatorship

Tactics: The Snow Vipers fight with barely controlled rage. They charge at the enemy, screaming and foaming at the mouth. The sight of this is sometimes enough to break up enemy formations, though more often, it merely serves as a way to "get the blood pumping" as Rallo would say.

Astiir negotiates all contracts, and she can be found during the summer months in the city of Jutensley. When a contract is accepted, she recruits who she can from the city's slums and dive bars. Other recruits come from the villages around the Lake of Ice, especially the ones who worship the Jute God of Murder above all others.

Logistics. Soldiers in the Snow Vipers are outfitted with **average** arms and equipment. Rallo is a frequent creator of minor magical items, especially ones who deal damage, maim, or destroy creatures. Because of this, roughly 40% of the Snow Vipers will own a personal common or uncommon magical item.

History. Little is known about the early years of the Snow Vipers. What is known is that Rallo Coldtounge was born somewhere around the Lake of Ice and was raised in a cult of demon worshipers. When he came of age and displayed a talent for magic, he was sent to live with a hermit who taught the child how to control his abilities.

He returned to his village sometime later and slew the head priest of the cult in a bid to take the group over. He killed any other opposition to his rule and converted the worship of the cult to that of Vemish, the Jute God of Murder and Blood. He enlisted the aid of a friend, Astiir, who was on the run from Jutan authorities for a series of murder-for-hire jobs she pulled off in the kingdom. Together, they began to teach rudimentary battle tactics to the back-water villagers in an attempt to forge them into a formidable fighting force. So far, the Snow Vipers have only taken contracts from some of the larger villages around the lake. One such contract had them pitted against the Darkblades of Jutan which in turn led to the severe wound suffered by Rallo, which also left him partially blind and deaf on his left side.

Notable NPCs: Lizardfolk Mercenary

LIZARDFOLK MERCENARY

Medium Humanoid (Lizardfolk), CE

ARMOR CLASS
15 (natural, shield)

HIT POINTS
28 (5d8+5)

SPEED
30 ft., Swim 30 ft.

| STR 15 (+2) | DEX 10 (+0) | CON 13 (+1) | INT 07 (-2) | WIS 12 (+1) | CHA 07 (-2) |

SKILLS
Perception +3, Stealth +4, Survival +5

SENSES
passive Perception 13

LANGUAGES
Draconic

CHALLENGE
1 (200 xp)

Disciplined. The lizardfolk mercenary has *advantage* on saving throws to resist the following condition: *charmed, frightened, stunned*.

Hold Breath. The lizardfolk mercenary can hold its breath for 15 minutes.

ACTIONS

Multiattack. Lizardfolk mercenaries make two melee attacks, each one with a different weapon.

Bite. *Melee Weapon Attack*: +4 to hit, reach 5 ft.; One target. Hit: 5 (1d6+2) piercing damage.

Heavy Club. *Melee Weapon Attack*: +4 to hit, reach ft.; One target. Hit: 5 (1d6+2) bludgeoning damage.

Spiked Shield. *Melee Weapon Attack*: +4 to hit, reach 5 ft.; One target. Hit: 5 (1d6+2) piercing damage.

EQUIPMENT

Spiked shield, heavy club, mercenary pack

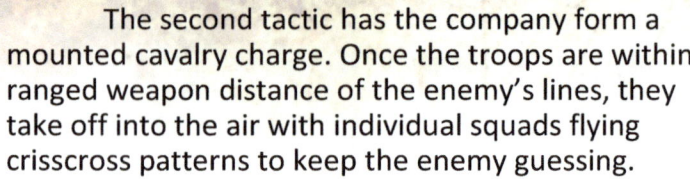

Name: Riders on the Storm

Nickname: Storm Riders, Winged Horsemen

Symbol: A pegasus facing sinister, on a blue, purple, or black field. Flown on banners and flags and displayed on shields.

Type: Standing/Fixed

Size: Troop; 50/10

Cost: 360 gp/185 gp/100 gp per week

Leader: Tenda Adoula (NG Human male Fighter 8)

Captain: 1; *Nala Mulinda (NG Human female Ranger 8)

Lieutenants: 2

Alignment: NG

Formation: The Riders consist of 50 *pegasus riders*.

Expertise: Single/Sustained Battle, War

Trustworthiness: 4

Base: Kalahga Preserve; Northern Savannah

Sphere of Operations: Northern Savannah, Desert of Urk

Government: Brotherhood Council

Tactics: The company routinely displays only two main battle tactics. The first consists of half of the riders staying aloft while shooting arrows at the enemy while the other half land and charge with heavy lances.

The second tactic has the company form a mounted cavalry charge. Once the troops are within ranged weapon distance of the enemy's lines, they take off into the air with individual squads flying crisscross patterns to keep the enemy guessing.

Logistics: The company gives **above average** weapons and armor to its soldiers. Each soldier is paired with a pegasus mount, and each individual soldier is responsible for the care of their mount. Potions and healing salves are given out before each battle. About 25% of the soldiers will have a personal common or uncommon magical item or weapon.

History: The Riders formed under the charismatic leadership of Tenda Adoula, a twenty-year veteran of the Kalahga Preserve Defense Force. Not content with just safeguarding the pegasus herds, Tenda wanted to form an aerial fighting force that had no rival. With the permission of the elders, he handpicked the first soldiers, making sure they were of good heart and always had the protection of the pegasus equal with the security of their own self.

Notable NPCs: Pegasus Rider

PEGASUS RIDER

Medium Humanoid (Human), NG

ARMOR CLASS
18 (scale mail, shield)
HIT POINTS
24 (4d8+4)
SPEED
30 ft.

STR	DEX	CON	INT	WIS	CHA
12 (+1)	14 (+2)	13 (+1)	11 (+0)	12 (+1)	13 (+1)

SKILLS Animal Handling +3, Perception +3
SENSES passive Perception 13
LANGUAGES Zualo
CHALLENGE 1 (200 xp)

Aerial Evasion. Whenever a pegasus rider succeeds on a Dexterity saving throw for half damage, they instead take 0 damage. This also applies to their mount.

Pinpoint Accuracy. The pegasus rider makes a critical strike with a ranged weapon on a roll of 19 or 20.

ACTIONS

Lance. *Melee Weapon Attack:* +3 to hit, reach 10 ft.; One target. Hit: 8 (1d12+1) piercing damage.

Morningstar. *Melee Weapon Attack:* +3 to hit, reach 5 ft.; One target. Hit: 6 (1d8+1) piercing damage.

Shortbow. *Ranged Weapon Attack:* +4 to hit, range 80/320 ft.; One target. Hit: 7 (1d6+2) piercing damage.

EQUIPMENT

Scale mail, shield, lance, morningstar, shortbow, quiver with 30 arrows, mercenary pack, military saddle, pouch of sugar cubes

PEGASUS

Large Celestial, CG

ARMOR CLASS
15 (barding)

HIT POINTS
59 (7d10+21)

SPEED
60 ft., Fly 90 ft.

STR 18 (+4) DEX 15 (+2) CON 16 (+3) INT 10 (+0) WIS 15 (+2) CHA 13 (+1)

SAVING THROWS Dexterity +4, Wisdom +4, Charisma +3
SKILLS Perception +6
SENSES passive Perception 16
LANGUAGES Understands Celestial, Zualo, Elvish, and Sylvan but cannot speak
CHALLENGE 2 (450 xp)

ACTIONS

Hooves. *Melee Weapon Attack:* +6 to hit, reach 5 ft.; One target. Hit: 11 (2d6+4) bludgeoning damage.

Name: *Ter Uddol* (The Crew)

Nickname: Metal Menagerie, The Company of Clicks and Whirls

Symbol: A pair of black gears, on a white or golden field. Worn on clothing and displayed on golems.

Type: Standing/Fixed

Size: Troop; 35/5

Cost: 1,000 gp/300 gp/100 gp per week

Leader: Sage Dursa *vas* Klondel (N Calvoid female †Technician 19)

Captains: 2; *Flormin *vor* Gordedon (LN Calvoid male Wizard 14), Poppolo *vor* Swervingen (LN Calvoid male Cleric 6/Wizard 6)

Lieutenants: 4

Alignment: LN

Formation: The Crew consists of 30 *mercenary wizards* and 5 *mercenary priests*. They, in turn, control 25 *basic guard units* and 5 *titan guardian units*.

Expertise: Guard Duty, Single/Sustained Battle

Trustworthiness: 5

Base: City of Kragum; Eastern Cliffs

Sphere of Operations: Eastern Cliffs, Verigal (Sylvar), Empire of Alteria (Zava Hills)

Government: Counseled Dictatorship

†*Technician described in Manastorm: World of Shin'ar*

53

Tactics: The tactics employed by the Crew are unique to their company's make-up. The automatons are lined up, with the BGUs in front of the TGUs. Behind them, the wizards and priests cast spells from relative safety. If the opposing force consists of large numbers of troops, the TGU's disintegration rays are used to thin the enemy's soldiers.

Dursa negotiates contracts herself, ensuring her troops earn top coin as befitting their magical expertise.

Logistics: The company grants **superb** equipment to its soldiers. With so much magical might, minor items such as potions and scrolls are readily available. Nearly 90% of the soldiers will have a personal common or uncommon magic item.

History: Two centuries ago, a group of Calvoid entrepreneurs formed the Crew from their collogues in the School of Law Keeping & Protection. At first, they acted as an unofficial arm of the Kragum security forces and were responsible for safeguarding travelers and merchants headed to the cliff-side city. Over time, the Crew began to take contracts from employers in other regions, most notably the city-states of Sylvar, in Verigal. There, they continued to wow onlookers with their noisy and sometimes comical march of battle-golems.

Dursa is the fourth elected leader of the Crew since its founding. She was voted in by the majority of soldiers, and she will hold the leadership position until she retires or until her death.

Notable NPCs: Basic Guard Unit, Titan Guardian Unit

BASIC GUARD UNIT
Medium Construct, Unaligned

ARMOR CLASS
19 (natural)
HIT POINTS
58 (4d10+20)
SPEED
20 ft.

STR 15 (+2)	DEX 14 (+2)	CON – (+0)	INT – (+0)	WIS 10 (+0)	CHA 02 (-4)

DAMAGE IMMUNITY Poison, psychic

CONDITION IMMUNITY Poisoned, blinded, deafened, charmed, exhaustion, frightened, paralyzed, petrified

DAMAGE VULNERABILITY Electricity

SENSES Darkvision 60 ft., Blindsight 60 ft., passive Perception 10

LANGUAGES Understands Calvish and Basic, but can only "speak" basic

CHALLENGE 4 (1,100 xp)

Charger. If the basic guard unit uses their action to Dash, they can use a bonus action to make one melee weapon attack or to shove a creature. If they move more than 10 feet in a straight line immediately before taking the bonus action, they can gain a +5 bonus to the attack's damage roll or push the target up to 10 feet away (if they choose to shove and succeed an attack roll).

Turtle. The basic guard unit can use its action to increase their AC for a short time by shrinking into itself, protecting vial joints and circuitry. While in this state, their AC increases by 4 points, but their movement speed is reduced to 10 feet. They can take no action except movement while in this state, and they can stay like this for a total of 8 minutes.

ACTIONS

Multiattack. The BGU can make two melee weapon attacks.

Shield Slam. Melee Weapon Attack: +4 to hit, reach 5 ft.; One target. Hit: 6 (1d6+2) bludgeoning damage.

Battleaxe. Melee Weapon Attack: +4 to hit, reach 5 ft.; One target. Hit: 7 (1d8+2) slashing damage.

TITAN GUARDIAN UNIT

Gargantuan Construct, Unaligned

ARMOR CLASS
24 (natural)

HIT POINTS
160 (14d20+30)

SPEED
10 ft.

STR 21 (+5) DEX 12 (+1) CON – (+0) INT – (+0) WIS 10 (+0) CHA 05 (-3)

DAMAGE IMMUNITY Poison, psychic

DAMAGE RESISTANCE Bludgeoning, piercing, slashing

CONDITION IMMUNITY Poisoned, blinded, deafened, charmed, exhaustion, frightened, paralyzed, petrified

DAMAGE VULNERABILITY
Electricity

SKILLS Perception +5

SENSES Darkvision 60 ft., Blindsight 60 ft., Tremorsense 120 ft., passive Perception 15

LANGUAGES Understands Calvish and Basic, but can only "speak" basic

CHALLENGE 14 (11,500 xp)

Alert. The titan guardian unit gains a +5 bonus to its initiative and it cannot be surprised. Creatures do not gain *advantage* on attack rolls against them as a result of being unseen.

Charger. If the titan guardian unit uses their action to Dash, they can use a bonus action to make one melee weapon attack or to shove a creature.

If they move more than 10 feet in a straight line immediately before taking the bonus action, they can gain a +5 bonus to the attack's damage roll or push the target up to 10 feet away (if they choose to shove and succeed an attack roll).

Sentinel. When the titan guardian unit hits a creature with an opportunity attack, the creature's speed is reduced to 0 for the rest of the turn. Creatures provoke opportunity attacks from the titan guardian unit even if they take the Disengage action. When a creature makes a melee weapon attack within 5 feet of a titan guardian unit, the TGU can use its reaction to make one melee weapon attack against that creature.

ACTIONS

Multiattack. The TGU makes three attacks with its mounted cannon. It can make two attacks with its arms and attempt to constrict, or it can make three slam attacks and forgo a constrict attempt.

Slam. *Melee Weapon Attack*: +10 to hit, reach 10 ft.; One target. Hit: 19 (2d12+5) bludgeoning damage.

Mounted Cannon. *Ranged Weapon Attack*: +6 to hit, range 20/60 ft.; One target. Hit: 23 (2d20+1) piercing damage.

Constrict. If the TGU succeeds in two slam attacks, they can attempt to constrict their target forcing it to make a DC 15 Dexterity saving throw. On a failed save, the target is *restrained* until the TGU releases it, or it breaks free. A creature can break free by succeeding on a Strength or Dexterity check against a DC 15 on their turn. The TGU cannot make melee weapon attacks while it is constricting a target.

Disintegration Ray (Recharge 6). *Ranged Weapon Attack*: +6 to hit, range 30/60 ft.; One target. Hit: 80 (10d6+40) force damage. If the damage reduces the target to 0 hit points; it is disintegrated.

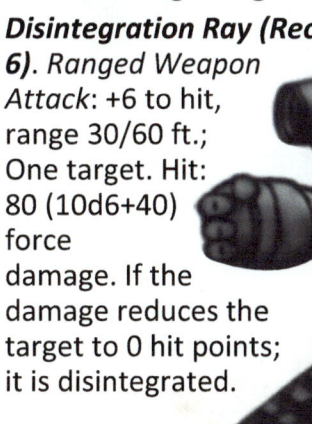

CHAPTER FOUR
MERCENARY SOLDIERS

TYPES OF MERCENARIES

Light Foot Soldier. The light foot soldier is one of the cheapest troops a mercenary company can muster and equip. Typically, they have very little formal training in martial combat beyond which end of the sword to point at the enemy. Sometimes, they include more disciplined soldiers, those that might have a modicum of combat experience.

Heavy Foot Soldier. The heavy foot soldier is the backbone of a mercenary company. Usually comprised of veteran troops, these soldiers include shock troops meant to overwhelm an enemy force. With more experience comes more responsibility, and the heavy foot soldier is often called on to keep the lesser soldiers in line.

Heavy Mounted Soldier. This soldier is a virtual powerhouse of combat power and experience. Most often decked out in heavy armor, a heavy mounted trooper is virtually unstoppable at full gallop. Expensive to house and maintain, only the wealthiest mercenary companies can afford to field heavy mounted soldiers.

Mounted Paladin. Very few who take the oath to become a paladin would ever consider joining a mercenary company. To make war and be paid to do it? But there are those who see fighting for a mercenary company as a holy venture. They accept payment but often donate most of it to a local shrine or temple dedicated to their deity.

Mounted Skirmisher. Lightly armored, the mounted skirmisher makes up for the lack of defense with increased mobility and lethality. Some mounted skirmishers act as calvary units, charging into a gap the foot soldiers may have opened. Others fire ranged weapons from the saddle, working as mobile artillery units and bringing death anywhere on the battlefield.

Mercenary Acolyte. The Gods speak to many different people, in many different lands. Some of those who hear the divine words find themselves in need of coin, and if their deity's dogma does not explicitly forbid it, they join a mercenary company. Sometimes they find themselves attached to a company to further their own personal doctrine.

Clerics of war gods especially hire on to mercenary companies.

Mercenary Ambusher. A more specialized trooper, the mercenary ambusher often lies in wait until the enemy is close enough to attack. Springing from concealed positions, they take advantage of the element of surprise to take out as many enemies as they can, as quickly as they can. Mercenary ambushers can also serve as advanced scouts and spies for their company, reporting back valuable information to their superiors.

Mercenary Archer. More often then naught, the mercenary archer joins a company already a master of ranged weapon combat. They may have been hunters, rangers, or local militia that trained daily with a bow or crossbow. They are generally lightly armored and are best positioned behind foot soldiers.

Mercenary Berserker. Rare are the soldiers who can work themselves into such a frenzy, that even their comrades give them a wide birth. Mercenary berserkers are the wild card of warfare. Savage and brutal, they possess a keen sense for all things combat-related. In times of peace, and back in camp, they can be at best a nuisance and at worst an unpredictable killer.

Mercenary Mage. Some wizards find themselves addicted to the rush of combat. They would rather be on the battlefield than in a tower lab or dusty library. The coin earned from spells cast keeps them happy, and the odd bit of magic lore then can gain from doing so, the better.

Mercenary Priest. These troops are few. There are not many who would dedicate their lives to both warcraft and a divine calling. Some mercenary priests stay out of combat, opting to stay behind the front lines and heal injured soldiers. Others yet join the fight willingly. They smite foes in the name of their deity and dedicate every win to their glory.

Mercenary Sorcerer. Similar to a mercenary wizard, the mercenary sorcerer joins a company for a regular paycheck. Some join to fuel their inflated egos. Tossing fireballs and ice storms on a battlefield, and getting paid to do it, is too intoxicating for some to pass up.

Mercenary Wizard. More than a mere dabbler in the arcane arts, the mercenary wizard sells power and talent to a company in exchange for steady coin. Most mercenary wizards do not stay with a company for long. The pursuit of knowledge sometimes outweighs the responsibility one has to commit to when expected to cast spells at a moment's notice.

MERCENARY ARMS & EQUIPMENT

The Tome of Mercenaries uses a scale that ranges from **poor** (lowest), to **average**, to **above average**, and finally to **superb** (highest) when discussing the types of weapons, armor, and general equipment the mercenary companies issue to their soldiers. Below is a series of tables listing what kind of equipment packages the GM can quickly add to a particular unit type, based on the above scale.

LIGHT FOOT SOLDIER

LOGISTICS LEVEL	SAMPLE EQUIPMENT
Poor	Padded armor, spear, dagger, shield
Average	Chain shirt, pike, shortsword
Above Average	Scale mail, shield, shortsword, dagger
Superb	Breastplate, shield, longsword, handaxe

HEAVY FOOT SOLDIER

LOGISTICS LEVEL	SAMPLE EQUIPMENT
Poor	Chain shirt, glaive, shortsword
Average	Scale mail, shield, dagger, warhammer
Above Average	Chain mail, shield, longsword, dagger
Superb	Splint mail, shield, longsword, handaxe

HEAVY MOUNTED SOLDIER

LOGISTICS LEVEL	SAMPLE EQUIPMENT
Poor	Chain shirt, spear, shield, shortsword, riding horse
Average	Breastplate, lance, war pick, shield, riding horse
Above Average	Chain mail, shield, lance, longsword, warhorse
Superb	Plate mail, lance, shield, longsword, warhorse

MOUNTED PALADIN

LOGISTICS LEVEL	SAMPLE EQUIPMENT
Poor	Chain shirt, longsword, shield, riding horse
Average	Breastplate, longsword, shield, riding horse
Above Average	Chain mail, lance, longsword, warhorse
Superb	Plate mail, lance, longsword, warhorse

MOUNTED SKIRMISHER

LOGISTICS LEVEL	SAMPLE EQUIPMENT
Poor	Leather armor, spear, sling, 20 bullets, riding horse
Average	Studded leather armor, shield, war pick, shortbow, 20 arrows, riding horse
Above Average	Chain shirt, spear, shield, 4 javelins , warhorse
Superb	Scale mail, shield, longsword, shortbow, 20 arrows, warhorse

MERCENARY AMBUSHER

LOGISTICS LEVEL	SAMPLE EQUIPMENT
Poor	Padded armor, shortsword, sling, 40 bullets
Average	Leather armor, shortsword, dagger, shortbow, 20 arrows
Above Average	Studded leather armor, shortsword, Light crossbow, 20 bolts
Superb	Studded leather armor, dagger, handaxe, heavy crossbow, 20 bolts

MERCENARY ARCHER

LOGISTICS LEVEL	SAMPLE EQUIPMENT
Poor	Padded armor, shortbow, 40 arrows, dagger
Average	Leather armor, shortbow, 40 arrows, mace
Above Average	Studded Leather armor, longbow, 40 arrows, shortsword
Superb	Chain shirt, longbow, 40 arrows, shortsword

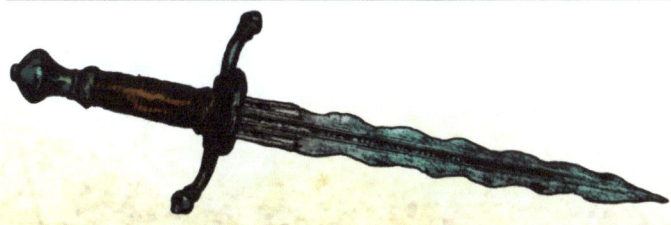

MERCENARY BERSERKER

LOGISTICS LEVEL	SAMPLE EQUIPMENT
Poor	greataxe, dagger
Average	Leather armor, shield, warhammer
Above Average	Hide armor, shield, handaxe, dagger
Superb	Scale mail, greataxe, 4 javelins

MERCENARY MAGE

LOGISTICS LEVEL	SAMPLE EQUIPMENT
Poor	Quarterstaff, 1 uncommon magical item
Average	Quarterstaff, 2 uncommon magical items, 1 rare magical item
Above Average	Dagger, 2 uncommon magical items, 1 rare magical item, wand of web
Superb	Dagger, 2 uncommon magical items, 1 rare magical item, *ring of protection, wand of fireballs*

MERCENARY PRIEST

LOGISTICS LEVEL	SAMPLE EQUIPMENT
Poor	Studded leather armor, shield, mace
Average	Chain shirt, shield, mace, potion of greater healing, 1 uncommon magical item
Above Average	Breastplate, flail, shield, *potion of greater healing*, 1 rare magical item
Superb	Chain mail, warhammer, shield, *potion of greater healing*, 1 rare magical item, *wand of paralysis*

MERCENARY SORCERER

LOGISTICS LEVEL	SAMPLE EQUIPMENT
Poor	Dagger, 1 uncommon magical item
Average	Dagger, sling, 20 bullets, 1 uncommon magical item
Above Average	Dagger, light crossbow, 20 bolts, 2 uncommon magical items
Superb	Dagger, 2 uncommon magical items, 1 rare magical item, *wand of lightning bolts*

MERCENARY WIZARD

LOGISTICS LEVEL	SAMPLE EQUIPMENT
Poor	Quarterstaff, 1 uncommon magical item
Average	Quarterstaff, 1 uncommon magical item, potion of flying
Above Average	Quarterstaff, 2 uncommon magical items, potion of flying, wand of magic missiles
Superb	Quarterstaff, 2 uncommon magical items, 1 rare magical item, *potion of flying, wand of binding*

NEW ITEM

Mercenary Pack (22 gp)

Includes a backpack, bedroll, crowbar, shovel, hammer, hooded lantern, 2 flasks of oil, mess kit, 10 pitons, iron pot, 10 days rations, sac, signal whistle, 10 iron spikes, tent, tinderbox, 10 torches, waterskin, whetstone, and a small knife.

LIGHT FOOT SOLDIER

Medium Humanoid (any), Any alignment

ARMOR CLASS
Varies

HIT POINTS
11 (2d8+2)

SPEED
30 ft.

STR 13 (+1) DEX 12 (+1) CON 12 (+1) INT 10 (+0) WIS 11 (+0) CHA 10 (+0)

SKILLS Athletics +3, Perception +2

SENSES passive Perception 12

LANGUAGES Any one language native to their race

CHALLENGE ¼ (50 xp)

Action Surge. On their turn, the light foot soldier can make one additional action on top of their regular action and a possible bonus action. They can do this once before a short or long rest.

HEAVY FOOT SOLDIER

Medium Humanoid (any), Any alignment

ARMOR CLASS
Varies

HIT POINTS
58 (9d8+18)

SPEED
30 ft.

STR 16 (+3) DEX 13 (+1) CON 14 (+2) INT 11 (+0) WIS 12 (+1) CHA 11 (+0)

SKILLS Athletics +5, Perception +2

SENSES passive Perception 12

LANGUAGES Any one language native to their race

CHALLENGE 3 (700 xp)

Action Surge. On their turn, the heavy foot soldier can make one additional action on top of their regular action and a possible bonus action. They can do this once before a short or long rest.

Combat Acumen. The heavy foot soldier gains a +1 bonus to their initiative and a +2 bonus to resist the *frightened* condition.

ACTIONS

Multiattack. The heavy foot soldier makes two melee weapon attacks.

REACTIONS

Parry. The heavy foot soldier adds 3 to its AC against one melee attack that would hit it. To do so, the heavy foot soldier must see the attacker and be wielding a melee weapon.

HEAVY MOUNTED SOLDIER

Medium Humanoid (any), Any alignment

ARMOR CLASS
Varies
HIT POINTS
52 (8d8+6)
SPEED
30 ft.

STR 16 (+3) DEX 11 (+0) CON 14 (+2) INT 11 (+0) WIS 12 (+1) CHA 14 (+2)

SKILLS Animal Handling +4, Perception +4

SENSES passive Perception 14

LANGUAGES Any one language native to their race

CHALLENGE 3 (700 xp)

Brave. The heavy mounted soldier has *advantage* on saving throws against being *frightened*.

Charge. If the heavy mounted soldier moves at least 30 feet straight toward a target then hits it with a melee weapon attack on the same turn, the target takes an extra 8 (2d6) damage.

Mounted Warrior. The heavy mounted soldier gains a +1 bonus to attack rolls while they are mounted.

ACTIONS

Multiattack. The heavy mounted soldier makes two melee weapon attacks.

MOUNTED PALADIN

Medium Humanoid (any), LG

ARMOR CLASS
Varies
HIT POINTS
52 (8d8+16)
SPEED
30 ft.

STR 16 (+3) DEX 11 (+0) CON 14 (+2) INT 11 (+0) WIS 14 (+2) CHA 16 (+3)

SAVING THROWS Constitution +4, Wisdom +4

SENSES passive Perception 12

LANGUAGES Any one language native to their race

CHALLENGE 3 (700 xp)

Brave. The mounted paladin has *advantage* on saving throws against being *frightened*.

Lay on Hands. The mounted paladin has a healing pool of 20 hit points they can use as their action to restore hit points to injured comrades.

Spellcasting. The mounted paladin is a level 4 spellcaster (DC 13, +5 to spell attacks).

Level 1 (3 slots): *bless, divine favor, wrathful smite*

MOUNTED SKIRMISHER

Medium Humanoid (any), Any alignment

ARMOR CLASS
Varies
HIT POINTS
27 (4d8+10)
SPEED
30 ft.

STR 13 (+1) DEX 15 (+2) CON 14 (+2) INT 12 (+1) WIS 12 (+1) CHA 10 (+0)

SKILLS Perception +3, Stealth +4

SENSES passive Perception 13

LANGUAGES Any one language native to their race

CHALLENGE 1 (200 xp)

Mounted Warrior. The mounted skirmisher gains a +1 bonus to attack rolls while they are mounted.

ACTIONS

Multiattack. The mounted skirmisher gets two melee or two ranged weapon attacks.

MERCENARY ACOLYTE

Medium Humanoid (any), Any alignment

ARMOR CLASS
Varies
HIT POINTS
11 (2d8+2)
SPEED
30 ft.

STR 11 (+0) DEX 11 (+0) CON 12 (+1) INT 11 (+0) WIS 16 (+3) CHA 13 (+1)

SKILLS Medicine +5, Religion +2
SENSES passive Perception 13
LANGUAGES Any one language native to their race
CHALLENGE ¼ (50 xp)

Spellcasting. The mercenary acolyte is a level 2 spellcaster (DC 13, +5 to spell attacks).
Cantrips (at will): *light, resistance, spare the dying*
Level 1 (3 slots): *cure wounds, guiding bolt, healing word*

MERCENARY ARCHER

Medium Humanoid (any), Any alignment

ARMOR CLASS
Varies
HIT POINTS
11 (2d8+2)
SPEED
30 ft.

STR 12 (+1) DEX 14 (+2) CON 12 (+1) INT 10 (+0) WIS 10 (+0) CHA 10 (+0)

SKILLS Perception +2
SENSES passive Perception 12
LANGUAGES Any one language native to their race
CHALLENGE ¼ (50 xp)

Archery. The mercenary archer gains a +2 bonus to attack rolls while wielding a ranged weapon.

MERCENARY AMBUSHER

Medium Humanoid (any), Any alignment

ARMOR CLASS
Varies
HIT POINTS
27 (6d8)
SPEED
30 ft.

STR 11 (+0) DEX 15 (+2) CON 10 (+0) INT 12 (+1) WIS 12 (+1) CHA 11 (+0)

SKILLS Perception +3, Stealth +4
SENSES passive Perception 13
LANGUAGES Any one language native to their race
CHALLENGE 1 (200 xp)

Ambush. The mercenary ambusher gains *advantage* on attack rolls against creatures who have not had their turn in combat yet.
Sneak Attack. Once per turn, the mercenary ambusher deals an extra 7 (2d6) damage when it hits a target with a weapon attack and has *advantage* on the attack roll, or when the target is within 5 feet of an ally of the mercenary ambusher does not have *disadvantage* on the attack roll.

MERCENARY BERSERKER

Medium Humanoid (any), Any Chaotic alignment

ARMOR CLASS
Varies
HIT POINTS
67 (9d8+27)
SPEED
30 ft.

STR 16 (+3) DEX 12 (+1) CON 17 (+3) INT 10 (+0) WIS 10 (+0) CHA 09 (-1)

SKILLS Athletics +5
SENSES passive Perception 10
LANGUAGES Any one language native to their race
CHALLENGE 2 (450 xp)

Danger Sense. The mercenary berserker gains *advantage* on Dexterity saving throws against effects that they can see. They lose this ability if they are ever *blinded*, *deafened*, or *incapacitated*.

Reckless. At the start of their turn, the mercenary berserker can gain *advantage* on all melee attack rolls during that turn, but attack rolls against it have *advantage* until the start of their next turn.

MERCENARY MAGE

Medium Humanoid (any), Any alignment

ARMOR CLASS
Varies
HIT POINTS
 40 (9d8)
SPEED
30 ft.

STR 09 (-1) DEX 14 (+2) CON 10 (+0) INT 18 (+4) WIS 12 (+1) CHA 11 (+0)

SKILLS Arcana +8, History +8
SENSES passive Perception 11
LANGUAGES Any Three
CHALLENGE 6 (2,300 xp)

Multiple Spellbooks. The mercenary mage has at least two spellbooks, one they take into combat, and one they leave back at camp.

Sculpt Spell. The mercenary mage can create pockets of safety within the effects of their spells. They can choose a number of creatures equal to 1 + the spell's level to automatically succeed on their saving throws against the spell cast. They take no damage if they would normally take half damage on a successful save.

Spellcasting. The mercenary mage is a level 9 spellcaster (DC 16, +8 to spell attacks).

Cantrips (at will): blade ward, fire bolt, light, minor illusion

Level 1 (4 slots): alarm, expeditious retreat, magic missile, witch bolt

Level 2 (3 slots): blindness/deafness, enlarge/reduce, hold person, scorching ray

Level 3 (3 slots): counterspell, dispel magic, fireball

Level 4 (3 slots): confusion, conjure minor elementals, fire shield

Level 5 (1 slot): wall of force

MERCENARY PRIEST

Medium Humanoid (any), Any alignment

ARMOR CLASS
Varies
HIT POINTS
 27 (5d8+5)
SPEED
30 ft.

STR 11 (+0) DEX 11 (+0) CON 12 (+1) INT 13 (+1) WIS 17 (+3) CHA 13 (+1)

SKILLS Medicine +6, Religion +4
SENSES passive Perception 13
LANGUAGES Any Two
CHALLENGE 2 (450 xp)

Grant Favor. The mercenary priest can use their bonus action to grant an ally a +2 bonus to their next attack roll, ability check, or saving throw. They can do this twice before a short or long rest.

Spellcasting. The mercenary priest is a level 5 spellcaster (DC 14, +6 to spell attacks).

Cantrips (at will): light, sacred flame, spare the dying

Level 1 (4 slots): bless, cure wounds, sanctuary, shield of faith

Level 2 (3 slots): enhance ability, hold person, prayer of healing

Level 3 (2 slots): dispel magic, revivify

MERCENARY SORCERER

Medium Humanoid (any), Any alignment

ARMOR CLASS
Varies
HIT POINTS
27 (5d8+5)
SPEED
30 ft.

STR 10 (+0) DEX 13 (+1) CON 12 (+1) INT 11 (+0) WIS 11 (+0) CHA 16 (+3)

SKILLS Arcana +2, Intimidation +5
SENSES passive Perception 10
LANGUAGES Any Two
CHALLENGE 4 (1,100 xp)

Sorcery Points. The mercenary sorcerer has 4 sorcery points to spend on abilities. They regain all spent points after a long rest.

Empower Spell. The mercenary sorcerer can spend 1 sorcery point to reroll a number of the damage dice in a spell they cast, up to 3. They must use the new rolls.

Heightened Spell. The mercenary sorcerer can spend 3 sorcery points to force a creature to save against a spell cast by them at a *disadvantage.*

Spellcasting. The mercenary sorcerer is a level 5 spellcaster (DC 14, +6 to spell attacks).

Cantrips (at will): acid splash, fire bolt, light, minor illusion, ray of frost
Level 1 (4 slots): burning hands, ray of sickness
Level 2 (3 slots): blur, web
Level 3 (2 slots):
fear, lightning bolt

MERCENARY WIZARD

Medium Humanoid (any), Any alignment

ARMOR CLASS
Varies
HIT POINTS
20 (4d8)
SPEED
30 ft.

STR 09 (-1) DEX 12 (+1) CON 10 (+0) INT 17 (+3) WIS 12 (+1) CHA 10 (+0)

SKILLS Arcana +5, History +5
SENSES passive Perception 11
LANGUAGES Any Three
CHALLENGE 3 (700 xp)

Multiple Spellbooks. The mercenary wizard has at least two spellbooks, one they take into combat, and one they leave back at camp.

Spellcasting. The mercenary wizard is a level 5 spellcaster (DC 14, +6 to spell attacks).

Cantrips (at will): blade ward, dancing lights, mage hand, shocking grasp
Level 1 (4 slots): chromatic orb, color spray, grease, sleep
Level 2 (3 slots): flaming sphere, levitate, misty step
Level 3 (2 slots): counterspell, fireball

APPENDIX A
ADVENTURING BANDS

A life on the road, delving into ancient ruins and bounding from rooftops, is alluring to some. Some long for a life filled with fighting monsters and vanquishing evil instead of sweeping up a temple basement. Others seek a kind of excitement that can only come from learning eldritch secrets from long-forgotten tombs.

No matter the reason for joining the life, adventurers are a peculiar lot. The famous and luckiest of them live to spin fantastic tales in taprooms across Shin'ar. Those types are few, and it is said you can count elderly adventurers in any region on one hand.

Below is a sampling of the types of adventuring companies that can be found all across the planet.

Name: Apallo's Talon

Leader: Apallo Glabus (NE Zevrish male Fighter 3)

Members: Moh Lanka (N Kalarin male Geomancer 3), Timait Turliko (CN Human female Cleric 2/Sorcerer 2), Meloch the Blade (NE Tiefling male Rogue 2)

Sphere of Operations: Empire of Alteria (Estanyan Plains, Zava Hills), Eastern Cliffs

Apallo Glabus is the son of a retired Senator from the city of Zor-Mal. He joined the Legions when he came of age, but his bad attitude and selfish nature got him kicked out before he could be deployed. He was given an honorable discharge, so his family name would not be sullied. His father subsequently kicked him out of his home with nothing but the shirt off his back.

Undismayed by his circumstances, Apallo used what remained of his connections to get a job bouncing at a dive bar. Weeks of busting noses and breaking up drunken brawls wore Apallo down, but he enjoyed his work.

He got to know a few regulars well, and when they asked him to join their forming adventuring band, he was quick to sign on. They made their way east to Bronzeville, hoping the ancient dragon Acri would sponsor them.

Along the way, Apallo got into a dispute with the group's leader. A fistfight quickly turned more dangerous as the other man pulled a small blade and stuck Apallo in the gut. Outraged that their compatriot would pull a weapon, the others in the group stepped in and overtook the armed assailant. They promptly booted him from their group, tied him up, and left him by the side of the road. Apallo was healed, and the group continued along their way. When they came to Bronzeville, they impressed the dragon enough that he named them a Talon, and gave them permission to stay in Bronzeville when not out adventuring. They have since traveled extensively around the Empire of Alteria and can currently be found searching ruins in the eastern Zava Hills.

APALLO GLABAS
Medium Humanoid (Zevrish), NE

ARMOR CLASS
16 (*breastplate +1*; 18 with shield)
HIT POINTS
28 (3d10+6)
SPEED
25 ft.

STR 16 (+3) DEX 12 (+1) CON 15 (+2) INT 11 (+0) WIS 13 (+1) CHA 11 (+0)

SAVING THROWS Strength +5, Constitution +4
DAMAGE RESISTANCE Poison
SKILLS Athletics +5, Intimidation +2, Perception +3, Survival +3
SENSES passive Perception 13
TOOLS Vehicles (land), playing cards
LANGUAGES Zavan, Alterian

Prone to Sickness. Apallo has *disadvantage* on saving throws to resist diseases.

Poison Resistance. Apallo has resistance to poison damage.

Combat Training. Apallo is proficient with martial weapons.

Fighting Style - Great Weapon. When Apallo rolls a 1 or 2 on a damage die for an attack with a melee weapon he is wielding in two hands, he can reroll the die, but he must use the new roll.

Second Wind. As an action, Apallo can heal

himself for 1d10+3 hit points. He can do this once before a short or long rest.

Action Surge. Apallo can take one additional action on top of his regular action once before a short or long rest.

Martial Archetype - Champion

Improved Critical. Apallo scores a critical strike on a roll of 19 or 20.

ACTIONS

Greatsword. *Melee Weapon Attack*: +5 to hit, reach 5 ft.; One target. Hit: 11 (2d6+3) slashing damage.

Battleaxe. *Melee Weapon Attack*: +5 to hit, reach 5 ft.; One target. Hit: 8 (1d8+3) slashing damage or 9 (1d10+3) slashing damage if used with two hands.

Javelin. *Melee or Ranged Weapon Attack*: +5 to hit, reach 5 feet, or range 30/120 ft.; One target. Hit: 7 (1d6+3) piercing damage.

EQUIPMENT

Breastplate +1, shield, greatsword, battleaxe, 4 javelins, explorer's pack, 3 flasks of oil, bullseye lantern, common clothes, belt pouch, playing cards, *potion of healing, potion of gaseous form, bracers of swimming & climbing*

Name: The Frozen Four

Leader: Journeyman Betrice *vas* Orvell from Politics & Religion (LN Calvoid female Wizard 10)

Members: Ragnar Vistok (LN Human male Anointed Knight 8 of Welkor), Joska of the Wolf (CN Rusk male Totemist 9), Duras Frosthair (LN Dwarf male Cleric 8)

Sphere of Operations: Northern Tip, Starfall Sea

The Frozen Four came together as a result of tragedy. Betrice *vas* Orvell and her husband arrived in Barrowtown from the city of Sparks to join the town's School of Politics & Religion. Betrice's husband was a sage who specialized in primitive religions, and he came to the Northern Tip to study the Rusk tribes. After two days in town, Betrice's husband was killed in a robbery attempt. The diminutive couple was accosted by thugs while they walked to a local inn to meet some new acquaintances for dinner that night.

Their dinner companions, a Rusk named Joska and his companion, Ragnar, were to meet them at the inn but were late, and managed to see the attack take place. They gave chase to the assailants, but could not catch them. Joska and Ragnar both swore an oath to avenge the attack. Ragnar paid for Betrice's husband's resurrection, but his soul would not leave the afterlife. Saddened, Betrice went into mourning. She sequestered herself away to use every divination she could think of to try and find his killer. Her magical scans paid off, and she enlisted the help of her new friends to make the trek to the city of Siimas with her.

They arrived in time to find the attacker holed up in an abandoned warehouse. The fight was fierce, leaving a number of the killer's allies dead and the killer himself taken back to Barrowtown in chains to face justice for his crime. Unwilling to return to her normal life without her husband, Betrice took an extended leave of absence from her School and formed the Frozen Four. The group travels between the communities of the Northern Tip, seeking those in need of the kind of justice that can only come from the tip of a sword. They have also earned the respect of the elusive Wolf tribe of Rusk for helping them eliminate a pack of demons that were harassing their hunting grounds.

BETRICE VAS ORVELL

Small Humanoid (Calvoid), LN

ARMOR CLASS
13 (*vest of defense*)

HIT POINTS
62 (10d6+20)

SPEED
25 ft.

STR 08 (-1) DEX 13 (+1) CON 15 (+2) INT 19 (+4) WIS 14 (+2) CHA 14 (+2)

SAVING THROWS Intelligence
+8, Wisdom +6

SKILLS Arcana +8, History +8, Insight
+6, Investigation +8

SENSES Darkvision 60 ft., passive
Perception 12

LANGUAGES Calvish,
Tradespeech, Juten, Alterian, Giant, Avar'urk, Draconic, Infernal

Magically Attuned. Betrice has *advantage* on Intelligence, Wisdom, and Charisma saving throws against magical spells. She is more susceptible to mana poisoning, and when she earns one mana poisoning point, she instead earns two.

Crystal Quality Control. Betrice has *advantage* on Intelligence (Investigation) checks to recognize the quality of refined and raw mana crystal.

Ritual Casting. Betrice can cast a wizard spell as a ritual if that spell has the ritual tag, and she has it copied into her spellbook without needing to prepare the spell.

Arcane Recovery. Once per day, when she finishes a short rest, Betrice can recover 5 spent spell slots of level 5 and below.

Arcane Tradition - Divination

Divination Savant. Betrice can copy divination spells into her spellbook for half the time and cost than other spells.

Portent. When Betrice finishes a long rest, she rolls two d20s and records the numbers. She can replace any attack roll, saving throw, or ability check made by her or a creature she can see with one of those rolls. She must choose to do so before the roll in this way only once per turn.

Expert Divination. When Betrice casts a divination spell of level 2 or higher using a spell slot, she regains one expended spell slot. The slot regained must be of a lower level than the spell cast, and it can't be higher than level 5.

The Third Eye. Betrice can use her action to summon increased powers of perception. She can choose one of the following that lasts until she takes a short or long rest.

- **Ethereal Sight.** Betrice can see into the Ethereal Plane within 60 feet.
- **Greater Comprehension.** Betrice can read any language.
- **See Invisibility.** Betrice can see invisible creatures and object within 10 feet and in her line of sight.

Keen Mind. Betrice always knows which way is North and how many hours are left before the next sunrise and sunset. She can accurately recall anything she has seen or heard within the past month.

Spellcasting. Betrice is a level 10 spellcaster. Her spellcasting ability is Intelligence (DC 16, +8 to spell attacks). She normally prepares the following 14 wizard spells.

Cantrips (at will): *blade ward, dancing lights, mage hand, minor illusion, ray of frost*

Level 1 (4 slots): *detect magic, feather fall, identify, magic missile*

Level 2 (3 slots): *detect thoughts, hold person, locate object*

Level 3 (3 slots): *clairvoyance, haste, sleet storm*

Level 4 (3 slots): *locate creature, polymorph*

Level 5 (2 slots): *mislead, scrying*

ACTIONS

Dagger +1. *Melee Weapon Attack*: +6 to hit, reach 5 ft.; One target. Hit: 6 (1d4+3) piercing damage.

EQUIPMENT

Dagger +1, *vest of defense*, scholar's pack, spell component pouch, belt pouch, common clothes, small steel mirror, *tan bag of tricks, goggles of adaptation, potion of greater healing, ring of feather falling, wand of web, staff of condensed mana*

NEW MAGICAL ITEM

Staff of Condensed Mana

Staff, very rare (requires attunement by a sorcerer, warlock, or wizard)

This staff has 10 charges. While holding it, you can use an action to expend 1 or more of its charges to cast one of the following spells from it, using your spell save DC and spellcasting ability modifier: *chromatic orb* (1 charge), *misty step* (2 charges), *hypnotic pattern* (3 charges), *stone shape* (4 charges), *telekinesis* (5 charges).

The staff regains 1d6+4 charges daily at dawn. If you expend the last charge, roll a d20. On a 1, the staff dissolves and releases the stored mana gas, giving every creature within 10 feet 1 mana poisoning point.

Each *staff of condensed mana* is different and unique; they will always have a single spell (from the sorcerer, warlock, or wizard spell lists), each from levels 1 through 5, chosen at random when the staff is created. Betrice's staff was created by her husband and contains the spells mentioned above.

Name: The Valkyries

Leader: Kilanna Flamehair (CG Human female Barbarian 12)

Members: Parvaneh *tel* Cyrio (CG Arryn female Bard 10), Yver Narldottor (CN Human female Warlock 9), Selina Raabe (CN Vampyr female Blade Dancer 9)

Sphere of Operations: Kingdom of Jutan, Empire of Alteria

Sometimes, adventurers just come together for the sheer thrill of things. Hap stances and coincidences are common on the road, and the formation of the Valkyries is no exception.

The Kingdom of Jutan has a number of ruins located in its southern Jarlands. The ruins are from an unknown race of people who are thought to have lived in the area centuries prior to the coming of the Jute.

Deep in one of those ruins, in a chamber, underground, Kilanna and her friend Yver found themselves at the mercy of a trio of devils that laired there. Just before one of the devils slit Yver's throat, it jerked back violently, and its head exploded with the impact of an enchanted crossbow bolt. Parvaneh and Selina found themselves lost in the same ruin, and happened to come across the scene while searching for a way out.

The fight was difficult even with help, but the four ladies managed to win the day. With a quick assurance that nobody would stab the other in the back, Kilanna and Yver led their rescuers out of the ruin. In debt to the pair, and a little bit smitten with Selina, Kilanna offered to take them to her home and cook them a hearty meal. The four ate and drank well into the night, and the next morning they all swore an oath to each other: friendship for life. The Valkyries can be found delving into ruins, fighting trolls in the Clawbite Hills, or punching chauvinistic men in tavern brawls.

KILANNA FLAMEHAIR

Medium Humanoid (Human - Jute), CG

ARMOR CLASS
14 (*hide +2*; 15 while dual wielding)

HIT POINTS
125 (12d12+36)

SPEED
30 ft.

STR	DEX	CON	INT	WIS	CHA
19 (+4)	11 (+0)	16 (+2)	12 (+1)	10 (+0)	14 (+2)

SAVING THROWS Strength +8, Constitution +9

SKILLS Athletics +8, Intimidation +6, Nature +4, Survival +4, Perception +4

SENSES passive Perception 14

TOOLS War Drums

LANGUAGES Juten, Tradespeech, Giant

Healthy Living. Kilanna has a +2 bonus to Constitution saving throws (already factored in).

Skilled. Kilanna is proficient with the Perception skill.

Rage. Kilanna can use her action to enter a rage in combat. While in a rage she gains the following benefits: resistance to bludgeoning, piercing, and slashing damage; advantage on Strength saving throws and ability checks; +3 damage on Strength-based melee weapon strikes. She can enter a rage 5 times per day.

Unarmored Defense. If Kilanna is wearing no armor, her AC is equal to 10 + her Dex modifier + her Con modifier. She can use a shield and still benefit from this ability.

Danger Sense. Kilanna has *advantage* on Dexterity saving throws against effects she can see.

Primal Path - Berserker

Frenzy. Whenever Kilanna is in a rage, she can also choose to be in a frenzy. While in this state, she can make a single melee weapon attack as a bonus action on each of her turns after entering the frenzy. If her rage ends while she was in a frenzy, she earns one level of exhaustion.

Mindless Rage. While Kilanna is in a rage, she cannot be *charmed* or *frightened*. If she was *charmed* or *frightened* when she enters a rage, the effect is suspended for the duration of the rage.

Intimidating Presence. Kilanna can use her action to frighten someone with her menacing presence. The creature must be within 30 feet and in her line of sight, and be able to hear her. It is allowed a Wisdom save against a DC 14 or be *frightened* of Kilanna until the end of her next turn. She can use her action again to extend the duration until the end of her next turn.

Dual Wielder. Kilanna gains a +1 bonus to her AC when wielding a weapon in both hands. She can dual wield weapons that do not have the light property, and she can stow or draw two weapons when she would typically be able to draw or stow just one.

ACTIONS

Multiattack. Kilanna makes two attacks when she takes the Attack action.

Battleaxe of Speed. *Melee Weapon Attack*: +10 to hit, reach 5 ft.; One target. Hit: 11 (1d8+6) slashing damage

Longsword +1. *Melee Weapon Attack*: +9 to hit, reach 5 ft.; One target. Hit: 10 (1d8+5) slashing damage.

Shortbow. *Ranged Weapon Attack*: +4 to hit, range 80/320 ft.; One target. Hit: 4 (1d6) piercing damage.

EQUIPMENT

Hide +2, battleaxe of speed, longsword +1, shortbow, quiver with 20 arrows, 2 *arrows +1*, explorer's pack, 1 vial of acid, common clothes, belt pouch, *boots of winterlands, potion of greater healing, potion of growth*

Name: Valiant Few

Leader: Alister Baxter (LG Frode male Paladin 16)

Members: Maalik *al*-Yameen (CG Sytash male Dervish 12), Laurr Alon'te (LN Illumnarus female Crystalmancer 15), Bree Tealeaf (CG Halfling female Sorcerer 13)

Sphere of Operations: Verigal, Southern Continent

The Valiant Few started out like most adventuring bands. A group of like-minded individuals answered a call to arms to help a beleaguered village fight off a tribe of goblins. After the battle, four of the volunteers stayed together and have traveled the world righting wrongs and exploring ancient ruins.

Their leader, Alister Baxter, is a self-imposed exile from his home in the Kingdom of the Flooded Forest. He won't speak of his past, other to say that he chose to leave his home rather than accept a decree given by his temple superior. His companions respect his privacy, though they have their guesses on what the order was perhaps pertaining too. The Church of Fro'kella is well known for being restricting in cases of love and marriage, and temple decrees given by high priests are treated as law in that kingdom.

ALISTER BAXTER

Small Humanoid (Frode), LG

ARMOR CLASS
19 (*half plate +2*; 21 with shield)

HIT POINTS
148 (16d10+48)

SPEED
25 ft.

STR	DEX	CON	INT	WIS	CHA
14 (+2)	16 (+3)	16 (+3)	12 (+1)	16 (+3)	17 (+3)

SAVING THROWS Wisdom +8, Charisma +8

SKILLS Athletics +7, Insight +8, Persuasion +8, Religion +6

SENSES passive Perception 13

LANGUAGES Froak, Meech, Tradespeech, Alterian

Augmented Healing. Alister gains 16 hit points after having a short rest.

Augmented Breathing. Alister can hold his breath for 10 minutes.

Agile Swimmer. Alister has *advantage* on Athletics checks made while swimming.

Pious Life. Alister gains a +3 bonus on attack and damage rolls against Undead creatures for 24 hours after he prays and fasts continuously for 12 hours.

Divine Sense. Alister can use his action to open his awareness to detect any celestial, fiend, or undead creature within 60 feet that is not behind total cover. He can do this 4 times before needing a long rest.

Lay on Hands. Alister has a well of 80 hit points to use to heal others with his touch.

Fighting Style - Protection. When a creature Alister can see attacks a target other than Alister that is within 5 feet of him, he can use his reaction to impose *disadvantage* on the attack. Alister must have a shield equipped to do so.

Improved Divine Smite. Alister can cause an extra 2d8 weapon damage + 1d8 radiant damage on targets if he uses a level 1 spell slot to augment the strike. The damage is increased by 1d8 for every spell slot above level 1 he uses. An additional 1d8 damage is applied if this is used on undead or fiends.

Divine Health. Alister is immune to disease.

Aura of Courage. Allies of Alister cannot be *frightened* if they are within 10 feet of him.

Cleansing Touch. Alister can use his action to end one spell on himself or on a willing creature. He can do this 3 times before needing a long rest.

Sacred Oath - Devotion

Channel Divinity. Alister can use his action to channel divinity and perform one of these actions:

- **Sacred Weapon**. Alister can imbue one weapon he is holding to strike with a +3 bonus. The weapon also sheds bright light and is considered magical.
- **Turn the Unholy**. Alister can present his holy symbol and attempt to turn a fiend or undead creature if they fail a Wisdom saving throw (DC 16). Turned creatures cannot come near Alister and must stay outside of 30 feet from him for the duration.

Aura of Devotion. Allies of Alister cannot be *charmed* if they are within 30 feet of him.

Purity of Spirit. Alister is always under the effects of a *protection from evil and good* spell. Aberrations, celestials, elementals, fey, fiends, and undead creatures have *disadvantage* on attack rolls against Alister.

Spellcasting. Alister is a level 16 spellcaster. His spellcasting ability is Charisma (DC 16, +8 to spell attacks). He has the following paladin spells readied:

Level 1 (4 slots): bless, cure wounds, heroism, shield of faith

Level 2 (3 slots): branding smite, zone of truth

Level 3 (3 slots): crusader's mantle, daylight, dispel magic

Level 4 (2 slots): aura of life, death ward

ACTIONS

Multiattack. Alister makes two attacks when he takes the Attack action.

Vicious Spear. *Melee Weapon Attack*: +7 to hit, reach 5 ft.; One target. Hit: 6 (1d6+2) piercing damage or 7 (1d8+2) piercing damage if used with two hands. If Alister rolls a natural 20 on an attack roll, the creature takes an additional 7 piercing damage.

Silver Shortsword. *Melee Weapon Attack*: +8 to hit, reach 5 ft.; One target. Hit: 7 (1d6+3) piercing damage or 14 points of piercing damage to creatures who are vulnerable to silver.

EQUIPMENT

Half plate +2, vicious spear, silver shortsword, priest's pack, 10 torches, 3 flasks of oil, 2 flasks of holy water, holy symbol, *helm of teleportation, potion of greater healing, pearl of power, ring of evasion, stone of good luck*

APPENDIX B
LEGENDARY COMPANIES

Name: The Company of Bones

Nickname: The Knights of the Sept, The Flayed Legion, countless others.

Symbol: A depiction of Caliban the Cruel, often woven or drawn on blood-soaked flayed skins.

Type: Recruiting/Roaming

Size: Legion; 401+ (varies)/250+

Cost: Each contract is different, but one thing is certain: the Company *always* demands a ritually binding blood oath and a single soul in return for their services. This is in addition to any monetary compensation.

Leader: Caliban the Cruel (NE Human [Ghoul] male Cleric 20 of the Sept)

Captains: 13; *Quartermaster Gemtooth (NE Deep Gnome [Lich] male Wizard 9/Rogue 8), *Badger Honeywhistle (NE Halfling [Vampire] male Rogue 15), Elijah (CG Aasimar male Paladin 9/Warlock 9), Buu (CN Drampyr male Shadowgiest 17), Nightscream (NE Young Adult Shadow Dragon [Gold Dragon] male), Abson "Sevenfold Arrow" (CN Tabaxi male Mystic 14), Brother Asura "Warhawk" (CN Human male Monk 12), Sardis "Bullet" (CN Aarakocra [Shade] male Gunslinger 12), Slade (LE Tiefling male Antipaladin 16), Micah Whisperrage (NE Human male Cleric 7/Warlock 6), Phelan Greywolf (CG Firbolg male Druid 15), Cyrek (LE Tiefling male Warlock 18), Ariolathon (N Half-elf male Ranger 9/Rogue 8)

Lieutenants: 6

Alignment: NE

Formation: The Company of Bones fields teeming hordes of undead, fiends, and other creatures alongside their forces, which swell with each slain foe. Their main body consists of both living and undead troops, with a cadre of priests and mages to maintain order. Extraplanar or specialized units are often led by one of the captains or their direct subordinates; all formations can vary in size and composition, depending on the conflict at hand.

Expertise: Guard Duty, Single/Sustained Battle, War

Trustworthiness: 5

Base: Citadel of 7 Sins; Khalas (Gehenna), The Black Gate/Caliban; Kingdom of Eltra (The Dark North), The Arena (Demiplane), numerous outposts scattered across the Planes.

Sphere of Operations: Multiplanar

Tactics: Caliban's forces are unpredictable, as they are not above using guerrilla warfare, espionage, assassination, extortion, or other means alongside highly organized and efficient formation - these are often backed by both heavy and light cavalry, siege weapons, magical support, and summoned creatures.

Logistics: Solders are equipped with **above average** arms and equipment. Every soldier is given a *potion of healing* before battle, as well as *potions of climbing* or similar magic, depending on the terrain and objective of the battle. Lieutenants are given magical versions of the weapons and armor that their unit uses. There is a 45% chance an individual soldier will have a common or uncommon magic item. Those in leadership positions often have numerous magical items at their disposal.

History: The origin of the Company of Bones is a tale filled with bloodshed, dark deeds, and black magic. The Sept, or Seven Sins, are a pantheon of sorts whose influence spreads from the depths of Gehenna to take root across the Planes. It is from a cult dedicated to the dark powers of the Sept that the Company began. As the cult grew, the need to protect itself from persecution did as well. This led to the formation of an order of dark knights sword to embrace the Sept's tenants and uphold their unholy writ. The Company of Bones first marched forth from Gehenna (through the use of a network of eldritch portals) in the wake of a cataclysmic event that shook the foundations of the Plane's first layer. Caliban's Fall, the conflict which cursed the founder with undeath, was the final act that cemented his rule in Gehenna. For a mortal (or rather, immortal undead) to reign in such a dark place, it required a bit of finesse. Caliban carved his way through the ranks of the infernal hierarchy, eventually assembling his own council, the Thirteen, which aided in controlling the Company's assets.

These individuals, both good and evil, embodied the Sept's ideals and would come to be as feared and respected throughout the Planes as their commander. The Company of Bones has served numerous causes, most notably the endless conflict known as the Blood War in which their members plied their bloody trade in exchange for gold, glory, and fresh souls. The Company earned its moniker for its macabre practice of using bits of bones, body parts, and other trophies from slain foes to decorate their equipment. Banners made from skinned enemies drip with unholy ichor, leaving a trail of blood and viscera in their wake.

They will offer their services to any willing to pay the price - a binding ritual, and offering of treasure accompanied by the sacrifice of a single soul. It is from these dammed souls that the Company's ranks swell - for the fallen are raised as undead, fiends, or used as currency among the planar entities that the Company deals with. Oddly enough, the Company of Bones has also served the cause of "greater good" by working alongside individuals and groups to wipe out threats to communities and/or organizations when those threatened could not protect themselves. Thus despite its 'evil' nature, it is often found employing celestials and other good-aligned creatures

who will not hesitate to dirty their hands in a confrontation.

Caliban the Cruel and the Thirteen fill a unique niche among the infernal hierarchy; while not fiends themselves, they have been recognized and accepted by such creatures for their tenacity and cunning on the battlefield, so much so that they are able to freely traffic their wares across the lower planes without fiendish opposition. Those who have faced the Company have one thing in common to say of them - there is no force more wicked, more depraved, or more valuable than the Sept's members in a fight. There is nothing they fear, nor anything that would break their loyalty. The Company's word is bond.

Each of their members has made an oath to serve in life and what comes after, for death is but a stepping stone which many in the ranks have overcome. From the Citadel of 7 Sins in Khalas, the Company makes use of portals that span the Planes, creating a web of gates that allows them to transport both troops and assets through magical means. One such portal, the Black Gate, is nestled deep in the heart of the Dark North. In the Kingdom of Eltra are a pair of obsidian obelisks towering roughly 300 feet amidst the mountains near the area known as the Boneyard and where that frozen place meets the Swamp of Skulls. It is here the Company of Bones makes its home on Shin'ar, as the Black Gate marks the entrance to a hidden city built within the bedrock of the mountains - Caliban. This place is the personificati on of the term 'Hell of Earth.' If one could imagine Hell as a flourishing underground city that thrived on the trade of slaves, souls, and dark magic.

Here, in the depths of the Dark North, is a haven where any vice can be found, and sin runs rampant. Murder, mayhem, and other dark deeds have become the status quo; anyone who can stomach such atrocities is welcome in Caliban - for it is said that anything can be found here, for the right price. Adventurers are able to come and go, as long as they abide by Caliban's (and by extension, the Sept's) laws. Any who fail to do so suffer the judgment of the Thirteen with the typical sentence handed out is undead servitude, slavery, or meeting a horrific end as decoration for Caliban's grisly architecture. Those bearing a Writ of Passage from the Thirteen or from Caliban himself are allowed to make use of their portals to travel far across Shin'ar and to other Planes, made possible by an extremely powerful artifact that enables Caliban to circumvent the laws of the Manasphere to disrupt its ban on extraplanar travel.

Notable NPCs: Leechtongue Ghoul, Leechtongue Lich, Leechtongue Swarm

GHOUL, LEECHTONGUE
Medium Undead, NE

ARMOR CLASS
14 (natural)

HIT POINTS
119 (17d8+34)

SPEED
30 ft.

STR 19 (+4) DEX 14 (+2) CON 15 (+2) INT 16 (+3) WIS 16 (+3) CHA 07 (-2)

SAVING THROWS Strength +8, Constitution +6, Wisdom +7

SKILLS Perception +6, Stealth +7

DAMAGE VULNERABILITY Fire, radiant

DAMAGE RESISTANCE Cold, necrotic; bludgeoning, piercing, and slashing damage from nonmagical attacks

CONDITION IMMUNITIES
Charmed, exhaustion, frightened, paralyzed, poisoned

SENSES Darkvision 60 ft., passive Perception 16

LANGUAGES Common, plus one language their progenitor chooses, Telepathy 50 ft.

CHALLENGE 12 (8,400 xp)

Daisychain Telepathy. A leechtongue ghoul who is within 50 feet of another leechtongue ghoul gains their telepathy distance in addition to their own.

Horrific Face. When the leechtongue ghoul's face is unseen, they appear as they did in life. When their face is visible, all creatures who gaze upon it must succeed on a DC 14 Wisdom saving throw or become *frightened* for 10 minutes. A successful save grants immunity to this feature for 24 hours. Creatures who succeed in the save three times in their life are immune to this feature permanently.

Spread. The leechtongue ghoul stores 1d4 Leechtongue Swarms, with a maximum of four swarms stored at any one time. It rejuvenates one swarm every third full meal it consumes.

ACTIONS

Multiattack. The leechtongue ghoul makes two attacks.

Unhinged Bite. *Melee Weapon Attack*: +8 to hit, reach 5 ft.; One target. Hit: 19 (3d10+4) piercing damage. If the target is a creature, it must succeed in a DC 14 Constitution saving throw or become poisoned for 10 minutes and take an additional 74 (5d12+2) necrotic damage.

Spew (ammunition per Spread feature). *Ranged Weapon Attack*: +6 to hit, range 30/60 ft.; One target. Hit: 14 (2d12+2) necrotic damage. On a successful hit, the target must succeed in a DC 14 Dexterity saving throw. On a failed save, a Leechtongue Swarm spawns on the target, already grappling them. On a successful save, the swarm spawns adjacent to the target.

LICH, LEECHTONGUE
Medium Undead, NE

ARMOR CLASS
20 (natural)

HIT POINTS
180 (19d8+95)

SPEED
30 ft.

STR 18 (+4) DEX 11 (+0) CON 20 (+5) INT 22 (+6) WIS 16 (+3) CHA 18 (+4)

SAVING THROWS Constitution +11, Intelligence +12, Wisdom +9, Charisma +10

SKILLS Arcana +12, Perception +9

DAMAGE VULNERABILITY Fire, radiant

DAMAGE RESISTANCE Cold, bludgeoning, piercing, and slashing from nonmagical attacks

DAMAGE IMMUNITIES Poison, necrotic

CONDITION IMMUNITIES Charmed, exhaustion, frightened, paralyzed, poisoned

SENSES Blindsight 120 ft., passive Perception 19

LANGUAGES Common, Infernal, Abyssal, Celestial, Telepathy 120 ft.

CHALLENGE 17 (18,000 xp)

Bolster Swarms. Creatures and swarms who have a leechtongue gain 5 temporary hit points while they are within 60 feet of a leechtongue lich. They can not benefit from this feature more than once in a 24 hour period.

Magic Resistance. The leechtongue lich gains *advantage* on saving throws against spells and other magical effects.

Leech Form. As a bonus action on their turn, or automatically upon reaching 0 hit points, the leechtongue lich may transform into a leechtongue swarm with 60 hit points and a movement speed of 30 feet. If at the time of the transformation, its lich form was below ½ of its hit point total, the lich form then regains 1d10 hit points every minute it is in the leech form until its lich form regains enough hit points to bring their current hit point total to exactly (or close to) ½ of its hit point total. If the leechtongue lich is reduced to 0 hit points while in leech form, the creature is considered destroyed, and it can not revert back to its lich form. Unless otherwise stated, this feature acts much in the same way as a druid's Wild Shape feature.

Spellcasting. The leechtongue lich is a level 19 spellcaster. Their spellcasting ability is Intelligence (spell save DC 20, +12 to spell attacks). They typically have the following spells prepared:

Cantrips (at will): *ray of frost, mage hand, chill touch*

Level 1 (4 slots): *magic missile, shield, ray of sickness*

Level 2 (3 slots): *invisibility, ray of enfeeblement*

Level 3 (3 slots): *animate dead, dispel magic, counterspell*

Level 4 (3 slots): *blight, fear*

Level 5 (3 slots): *cloudkill, scrying*

Level 6 (2 slots): *disintegrate*

Level 7 (1 slot): *finger of death*

Level 8 (1 slot): *power word stun*

Level 9 (1 slot): *time stop*

ACTIONS

Multiattack. The leechtongue lich makes two melee weapon attacks or one melee attack, and one ranged attack.

Staff of Rotting. *Melee Weapon Attack*: +12 to hit, reach 5 ft.; One target. Hit:11 (1d8+6) bludgeoning damage plus 22 (4d8+2) necrotic damage.

Rotting Bolt. *Ranged Weapon Attack*: +8 to hit, range 60/120 ft.; One target. Hit: 22 (4d8+2) necrotic damage. If the target is a creature, they must succeed in a DC 14 Constitution saving throw or be *poisoned* for 10 minutes.

NEW MAGICAL ITEM

Staff of Rotting

Staff, very rare (requires attunement by a spellcaster)

This staff can be wielded as a magic quarterstaff that grants a +2 bonus to attack and damage rolls made with it. When the staff successfully strikes a target, it blasts the target with necrotic energy, dealing an additional 22 (4d8+2) necrotic damage with every blow.

Rotting Bolt. The staff can be made to shoot a bolt of necrotic energy, dealing 22 (4d8+2) necrotic damage on a successful strike. In addition, if the target is a creature, they must succeed in a DC 14 Constitution saving throw or earn the *poisoned* condition for 10 minutes.

SWARM, LEECHTONGUE

Swarm of Tiny Undead, NE

ARMOR CLASS
15

HIT POINTS
35 (8d4+16)

SPEED
15 ft.

STR 11 (+0) DEX 20 (+5) CON 14 (+2) INT 04 (-3) WIS 12 (+1) CHA 07 (-2)

DAMAGE RESISTANCE Bludgeoning, piercing, and slashing from nonmagical weapons

SENSES Darkvision 60 ft., passive Perception 11

LANGUAGES Cannot speak; Telepathy 30 ft.

CHALLENGE 3 (700 xp)

Parasite. When a creature a leechtongue swarm is grappling is reduced to 0 hit points, the swarm consumes and replaces its tongue, transforming it into a single leechtongue that then joins the swarm. It can also consume and transform the tongue of a creature who has been stabilized but has not yet regained any hit points, if that creature fails a DC 14 Constitution saving throw.

Swarm. Leechtongue swarms can occupy the space of another creature, and they can squeeze into any opening large enough to fit a quipper. The swarm can not regain lost hit points or gain temporary hit points unless the temporary hit points are from a leechtongue lich's Bolster Swarm feature.

ACTIONS

Overwhelm. *Melee Weapon Attack:* +7 to hit, reach 0 ft.; One creature that occupies the same space as the Swarm. Hit: 16 (4d6) piercing damage or 8 (2d6) piercing damage if the swarm has less than ½ of its total hit points remaining. The creature must succeed in a DC 14 Strength or Dexterity (their choice) saving throw or become grappled by the swarm.

Twisted Origins. After Caliban's transformation, he went about creating servants who would help fulfill his dreams of domination. Using dark magic rituals, he created the first leechtongue swarms and unleashed them in several places, including the planet of Shin'ar. Next, he transformed a group of powerful spellcasters, most of which were former or current apprentices of his, into leechtongue liches. These beings followed their master's decent into Gehenna and work with the Sept's priesthood to control the Company's undead and fiendish rabble.

All Consuming Hunter. Like the blood-sucking swarms that they unleash, leechtongue ghouls thrive in places where they can feed indiscriminately, such as underground caverns, crypts, or dark alleyways near cemeteries. When they can't feed on the dead, they pursue living creatures and spawn leechtongue swarms as much as possible. A leechtongue ghoul's flesh does not rot, and the creature can persist in a crypt of tomb for untold ages without feeding. Caliban the Cruel "rewards" elite troops within the Company of Bones by infecting them with leechtongue swarms so they can continue their fight, even after death.

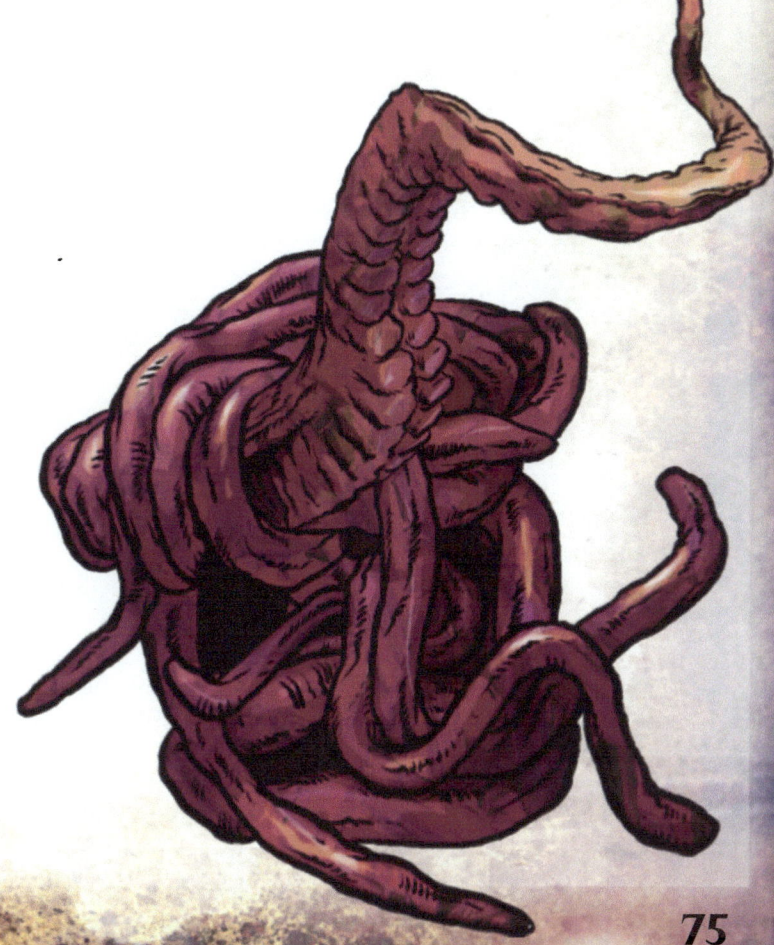

Name: The Most Illustrious Knights of the Order of *Drakonem Exterminatus*, Defenders of the Southern Reach & It's Lands And Bounties

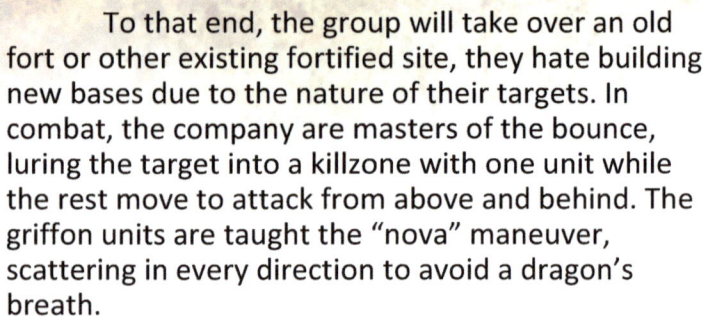

Nickname: The Dragonslayers, Scalebreakers

Symbol: Three winged blades, pointing downwards.

Type: Standing (Recruiting)/Fixed

Size: Battalion; 95 (125)/100

Cost: 1250 gp/120 gp/300 gp

Leader: Sir Kyto-su du Locke*

Captains: 4; Dradus (LN Human male Fighter 15), Tana (N Half-elf Fighter 10/Ranger 5), Hrest (LG Tiefling male Paladin 15), Minevra (CG Aasimar female Ranger 15)

> ** Kyto-su du Locke does not exist. The captains take turns wearing the armor of Kyto-su du Locke while negotiating contracts.*

Lieutenants: 16

Alignment: LN

Formation: The main contingent of the Dragonslayers is a group of 45 *elite griffon knights*, ten to each squad with five in reserve. They are backed up by a trained cadre of three heavy artillery units of ten men each. They recruit from the local population if needed, fielding these as *mercenary archers* or *ambushers*. The remaining members are split between 10 *mercenary priests* and 10 *mercenary wizards*. Because of their chosen target, all who join are proficient with the shortbow, longbow, and crossbow.

Expertise: Guard Duty, Single/Sustained Battle

Trustworthiness: 5

Base: The Eyrie Impregnable; Aderia Mountains, Verigal

Sphere of Operations: Verigal (Esta, The Handle, Sylvar)

Government: Brotherhood Council

Tactics: While defending, the Dragonslayers bring in heavy equipment, such as ballista, and work with clients to prepare them for dragon attacks. They're very efficient at setting up quickly, but also have a tendency of adding that to their bill with every fortification their men instruct in.

To that end, the group will take over an old fort or other existing fortified site, they hate building new bases due to the nature of their targets. In combat, the company are masters of the bounce, luring the target into a killzone with one unit while the rest move to attack from above and behind. The griffon units are taught the "nova" maneuver, scattering in every direction to avoid a dragon's breath.

Logistics: The company is outfitted with **superb** arms and equipment. The main tool of the company are the griffons themselves. Griffons take at least three years to become mature enough to ride, and their eggs can be quite rare. The Order's base is a natural spire and griffon hatchery, and mature griffons and new riders are trained there. Most of the griffon knights are armed with a lance, shield, and shortbow. Lieutenants are often given *arrows of dragon slaying* and the magical units take up most of their time creating the deadly ammunition.

History: The beginnings of the company go back to the Barony of du Locke, outside the City-State of Hortta, and its destruction by dragon fire 300 years ago. The sole survivor, a wood elf foundling taken in by the du Locke family, sought aid from the nearby estates and towns but was rejected. Emboldened by the rejections, and calling himself Kyto-su du Locke, he began forming a free company of down-on-their-luck warriors and began throwing them at every dragon lair and territory dispute with dragons he could find. Eventually, the order won fame and coin, enough to buy Kyto-su a title and his growing company a base where they could train their griffons.

Du Locke's death was a product of his personal vendetta against the dragon who destroyed his home, *Gil'cro'tanax the Red*. They met in the heart of a dormant volcano and slew each other in an epic battle of sorcery and steel. The company did not lose its charismatic leader that day, even though his body could not be resurrected. Instead, du Locke's captains took his fire-scorched armor and preserved it, as a symbol of the man who took a bunch of nobodies and renegades and molded them into a force of professional warriors and knights.

Since then, the ruling council of captains has kept the legend of Sir Kyto-su du Locke alive, scarred and deformed by his quest against dragonkind, but possessing a spirit full of courage and bravery.

Notable NPCs: Elite Griffon Knight

ELITE GRIFFON KNIGHT

Medium Humanoid (any), LN

ARMOR CLASS
20 (plate mail, shield)

HIT POINTS
90 (12d8+36)

SPEED
30 ft.

STR 16 (+3) DEX 16 (+3) CON 16 (+3) INT 10 (+0) WIS 12 (+1) CHA 10 (+0)

SAVING THROWS Strength +4, Dexterity +6

SKILLS Animal Handling +7, Athletics +6, Perception +4

SENSES passive Perception 14

LANGUAGES Veri'urk, Tradespeech, Lumnar, Elvish

CHALLENGE 5 (1,800 xp)

Emergency Landing. Elite griffon knights wear a magic ring through which they can cast the spell *feather fall* on themselves, once, as a reaction to falling from a great height. Once the stored spell is cast this way, the ring becomes inert until five days have passed.

Mounted Aerial Combatant. If an elite griffon knight is not *incapacitated* and they are mounted upon a griffon, they gain the following benefits:

- The elite griffon knight has *advantage* on melee attack rolls against un-mounted creatures that are smaller than their mount.
- The elite griffon knight can use their reaction to force an attack targeted at their mount to target them instead.
- If the elite griffon knight's mount is subjected to an effect that allows it to make a Dexterity saving throw to take only half damage, it instead takes no damage if the save succeeds and only half damage if the saving throw fails.

ACTIONS

Multiattack. The elite griffon knight makes three attacks using either their lance or their shortbow.

Lance. *Melee Weapon Attack*: +6 to hit, reach 10 ft.; One target. Hit : 9 (1d12+3) piercing damage.

Shortbow. *Ranged Weapon Attack*: +6 to hit, range 80/320 ft.; One target. Hit: 6 (1d6+3) piercing damage.

Variant: Shortbow w/Dragonslayer Arrow. *Ranged Weapon Attack*: +6 to hit, range 80/3210 ft.; One target. Hit: 6 (1d6+3) piercing damage. If the target is of the dragon type, they must make a DC 17 Wisdom saving throw or take an additional 6d10 magical piercing damage.

REACTION

Nova. While mounted, the elite griffon knight may force their mount to use up to 10 feet of movement to evade a line, cone, or sphere of some type of damaging effect (like dragon breath), as a reaction. This movement may occur even if they are not able to evacuate the damaging space, and is subtracted from their next round's movement.

EQUIPMENT

Plate mail, shield, lance, shortbow, quiver with 40 arrows, mercenary pack, military saddle, *ring of emergency landing*

NEW MAGICAL ITEM

Ring of Emergency Landing

Wondrous item, uncommon

This plain ring of bronze is stamped with the symbol of the mercenary company known as the Dragonslayers, and is not often seen in the hands of non-members. Stored in the ring is a single casting of the spell *feather fall*, and the magic of the ring allows the spell to be cast as a reaction by the wearer of the ring. Once cast, the ring itself becomes inert while its magic slowly replenishes over the course of five days.

These rings are issued to the mercenary company's elite griffon knights. Once used, a knight can swap their ring out for a functioning one at the company's base of operations.

Name: Peasants and Farmers

Nickname: Farmers

Symbol: A red shovel and hoe in an X configuration, often on a blue background.

Type: Recruiting/Fixed

Size: Legion; 250 (250)/200

Cost: 2000 gp/25 gp per day per soldier and 30 gp per day per mounted soldier/No weekly fees

Leader: Commander Sarskel Coveto (NG Human male Cleric 9)

Captains: 2; *Sarion Stargale (NG Human male Ranger 6), Kenneth McCormick (LN Human male Fighter 5)

Lieutenants: 2

Alignment: N

Formation: The Farmers have been able to field an impressive 200 *light foot* and 100 *Greenthumb Phalanx* on the battlefield. They are accompanied by two separate battalions of 100 soldiers each, made up of *heavy mounted* troops and *mercenary archers*.

Expertise: War

Trustworthiness: 4

Base: Goldenfields (fortified land and keep); the Northern Savanna

Sphere of Operations: The Northern Savanna, Verigal (Esta, Sylvar), The Barren Islands

Government: Council

Tactics: Commander Coveto will often demand parlay from an opposing force after he carefully arranges his troops on the battlefield. He rides out with his captains, full honor-guard, and standard bearers. He will insist the opposing commander hears his terms of surrender, and gives exactly 12 hours to respond. He only gives this offer once. If and when combat is engaged, his soldiers fight with well-practiced tactics and formation that could be textbook examples taught at the best war colleges.

Logistics: The company is outfitted with **above average** arms and equipment. Mounted soldiers all carry lances, and archers are trained with a composite-type longbow, granting them greater mobility on the battlefield. All soldiers also carry either a shovel or hoe, as a symbol of their company and also as a weapon, if needed.

History: A half-century ago, a string of small farming communities were established in the Northern Savanna by people not native to the land. Most came from the Western Shore, but others hailed from Verigal and the Zava Hills. They were attracted by the fertile, but inhospitable, lands, and some were sent as secret envoys to establish settlements friendly to foreign powers. After a time clearing the disorganized monstrous tribes and vermin, the lands were tilled and the first crops were planted.

After a bountiful harvest, the fledgling communities were attacked by a large horde of Gnolls. The farmer's meager defenses were no match for so many, and the farms and homesteads were overrun, looted, and destroyed. A young priest named Sarskel Coveto helped organize a large group of fleeing survivors, and with whatever weapons they could find, managed to hold off enough Gnolls for more refugees to make it to safety.

After resting for a short while, Sarskel and his troop of farmers-turned-soldiers rallied more survivors and they went back to the destroyed farms. Death and utter destruction greeted them, and they managed to only find a single survivor, a young boy named Kenneth McCormick.

The Gnolls would not come back that day, and the survivors were free to try and rebuild what they could. Learning from their past mistakes, they focused on defense and training. A full decade would pass before the communities were again threatened by anything larger than a passing warband. In that time, Sarskel Coveto, now calling himself Commander, managed to mold the farmers into a force of well trained and disciplined soldiers. When not protecting the lands they control, the Farmers take contracts elsewhere, with most of the earned coin going right back to the defense and upkeep of their shared community.

Notable NPCs: *Greenthumb Phalanx*

GREENTHUMB PHALANX

Medium Humanoid (any), N

ARMOR CLASS
17 (scale mail, shield)

HIT POINTS
35 (4d8+8)

SPEED
30 ft.

STR 16 (+3) DEX 12 (+1) CON 14 (+2) INT 10 (+0) WIS 12 (+1) CHA 10 (+0)

SKILLS Athletics +5, Intimidation +2, Perception +3, Survival +3

SENSES passive Perception 13

LANGUAGES Zualo, Tradespeech

CHALLENGE 2 (450 xp)

Action Surge. Greenthumb Phalanx can take one additional action on top of their regular action once before a short or long rest.

Lock Shields. As a bonus action, a Greenthumb Phalanx can lock their shields in a way that offers a +2 bonus to an ally's AC, if that ally is situated to the Greenthumb Phalanx's left side and if the Greenthumb Phalanx is standing next to another Greenthumb Phalanx who is also using their Lock Shields ability. The AC bonus lasts for 2 rounds + 1 round per Constitution modifier of the Greenthumb Phalanx.

Set For Charge. Using their action, a Greenthumb Phalanx can set their one-handed guisarme in a way that enables it to deal triple damage against a mounted target that charges (moves at least 30 feet) towards the Greenthumb Phalanx and makes a melee attack. The retaliatory attack is triggered by the mounted charge, and gains a +3 bonus to hit. Once set this way, the Greenthumb Phalanx can maintain this position indefinitely, and can use a bonus action to un-set their weapon. While their weapon is set this way, their movement speed is reduced to 0. A Greenthumb Phalanx cannot use their Lock Shields ability if they are set to receive a charge.

ACTIONS

One Handed Guisarme. *Melee Weapon Attack:* +5 to hit, reach 10 ft.; One target. Hit : 9 (1d10+3) piercing damage.

EQUIPMENT

Scale mail, shield, one-handed guisarme, mercenary pack

NEW WEAPON

Name	Cost	Damage	Weight	Properties
One-handed Guisarme	15 gp	1d10 piercing	3 lb.	Reach

Name: Blood Ravens

Nickname: Ravens

Symbol: A black kite shield with the silhouette of a red raven with open wings. The symbol is not openly worn by the company's members.

Type: Standing/Fixed

Size: Troop; 30

Cost: 1300 gp/No daily fees/No weekly fees; the Blood Ravens take additional payments in slaves, lands, and titles.

Leader: Master Lesh Moon (NE Zevrish male Cleric 9)

Captains: 1; *Maree Black (NE Zevrish female Monk 9)

Lieutenants: 1

Alignment: NE

Formation: The Ravens' main force consists of 15 *Frontline Fanatics*, who are in turn backed up by 10 *mercenary archers*, 2 *mercenary priests*, 2 *mercenary sorcerers*, and a single *mercenary ambusher*.

Expertise: Single/Sustained Battle

Trustworthiness: 2

Base: Blood Raven Keep; Zava Hills

Sphere of Operations: Empire of Alteria (Zava Hills), The Barren Islands

Government: Theocratic Dictatorship

Tactics: The Ravens make use of subterfuge, sabotage, and assassinations on enemy command structures. They rarely meet opposing companies in battle, preferring instead to dismantle and demoralize their enemies before a battle is even started.

Logistics: The company is outfitted with **average** equipment. Potions and minor magical items that enhance stealth are available to any soldier before embarking on a mission.

History: Master Lesh Moon's heart belongs to Brhuaal. After receiving a dream vision from his god, Lesh went about preaching in the back alleys of Zevrish cities and towns. His sermons consisted of hate-filled monologues and fiery speeches calling for the armed attack on weak-minded individuals who would rather live peacefully than sow chaos and death. He was paid no mind, at first. Slowly, he began to accumulate enough followers to give the authorities pause. Especially considering the type of people he was attracting.

Lesh understood that to really change the course of history you need power, and power comes from action and influence. Backing off from street corner demagoguery, Lesh began to seek similar minded individuals in positions of power, and then offer the services of himself and his new band of fanatical ruffians.

The Blood Ravens have been slowly earning coin and lands thanks to the hostile political climate found in the Zava Hills. Raids by the Ravens on homesteads, villages, and merchant caravans have earned them the hatred of many. Lesh cares not for the opinions of future slaves, and only seeks to continue his reign of chaos long enough to inflict as much pain as possible on those who scoff at or fear the Darkness, and all that it brings.

Notable NPCs: *Frontline Fanatic*

FRONTLINE FANATIC

Medium Humanoid (Zevrish), NE

ARMOR CLASS
14 (ring mail)
HIT POINTS
58 (9d8+18)
SPEED
25 ft.

STR 16 (+3)	DEX 10 (+0)	CON 14 (+2)	INT 10 (+0)	WIS 10 (+0)	CHA 09 (-1)

SKILLS Athletics +6, Intimidation +2, Perception +3, Survival +3
SENSES passive Perception 13
LANGUAGES Zavan, Alterian
CHALLENGE 3 (700 xp)

Improved Critical. Frontline Fanatics score a critical strike on a roll of 19 or 20.

Relentless Hate. If a Frontline Fanatic is brought to 0 hit points, and before death saving throws are rolled, they are allowed a single Constitution saving throw against a DC 20. If successful, the Frontline Fanatic does not drop to 0 hit points and instead heals for 1d10 hit points + their Constitution modifier. If the saving throw fails, the Frontline Fanatic earns two death saves. Frontline Fanatics can only benefit from this feature once in a 72 hour period.

Shadow Step. Using their action, Frontline Fanatics can enter a medium sized shadow, including their own, and materialize from another medium sized shadow within 60 feet of their position. They may do this once before a short rest.

ACTIONS

Multiattack. Frontline Fanatics make two greatsword attacks, or they can throw two handaxes.

Greatsword. *Melee Weapon Attack*: +6 to hit, reach 5 ft.; One target. Hit: 11 (2d6+3) slashing damage.

Handaxe. *Melee Weapon Attack*: +6 to hit, reach 5 feet or range 20/60 ft.; One target. Hit: 7 (1d6+3) slashing damage.

EQUIPMENT

Ring mail, greatsword, 4 handaxes, mercenary pack, holy symbol (Brhuaal)

Name: Mosscale Legion
Nickname: Green Scales
Symbol: A stylized Kobold skull with a tree on top. Shown on surcoats, shields, and flags.
Type: Standing/Fixed
Size: Legion; 400/200
Cost: 1500 gp/200 gp/250 gp per week
Leader: Svant di Caesin (NE Kobold male Fighter 5)
Captains: 10; *The Yowelt Caesin (a group of veteran fighters who answer directly to Svant)

Lieutenants: 12

Alignment: NE

Formation: The vast majority of troops in the legion are *light foot*, and they number 300. They are broken into smaller units, ranging from 9 to 19 soldiers per unit, and led by a *heavy foot soldier*, of which there are 60. A force of 30 *mercenary archers* and 10 *mercenary sorcerers* make up the rest of the legion.

Expertise: Guard Duty, Single/Sustained Battle, War

Trustworthiness: 3

Base: Mosscale Castle; Arryas Mountains

Sphere of Operations: Arryas Mountains, Empire of Alteria (Zava Hills), Damp Forest

Government: Military Dictatorship

Tactics: The company's tactics can vary depending on the contract they are assigned. Kobolds of the legion act against type, and are as courageous and brave as other mercenary soldiers. They are often underestimated in battle, and they use this to their advantage.

Logistics. The company's troops are outfitted with **average** arms and equipment. Svant di Caesin learned early that poor equipment can be a deciding factor in war. Very few soldiers will have a personal magical item, though potions are readily available upon request.

History. Kobolds are not native to the planet of Shin'ar. Over the eons since Lunar Quickenings began depositing people on the world, very few of that species have found themselves marooned on the unique planet. A decade ago, high in the Arryas Mountains, a large portal opened to an underground city that was in the middle of a civil war. The beings who controlled the city were elves who were malicious and evil. They enslaved countless species, and put them against each other in weekly war games and gladiator matches. Those who displeased them were sacrificed to their spider goddess.

During the civil war, many slaves found themselves free from their owners. A large group of Kobold soldiers who were hiding from their master's killers, came upon the portal to Shin'ar and took a chance at a new life in a new place. Not all of the slave-soldiers made it through the portal before it closed, including the family of their leader, Svant di Caesin.

Svant went about organizing his troops, who all looked to him for guidance during this time. Weeks would go by before the Kobolds would come into contact with other intelligent species, most notably the Arryn people. Instead of sending troops to deal with the large gathering of seemingly well-armed interlopers, a delegation from the Ruling Family suggested the Kobolds relocate closer to the base of the mountains.

With help from the Arryns, the Kobolds took over an old Zevrish fort and began to settle down in their new home. Soon, Mosscale Legion soldiers could be found guarding warehouses and caravans. They have been contracted eight times by the city of Pursa to eradicate rampaging Goblins and other vermin from the city's territory. The Legion has since taken other contracts outside of the Arryas Mountains, most notably guarding caravans through the Zava Hills and battling Drazil in the Damp Forest.

Name: The Devil's Nightmare Regiment (*Das TeufelsAlpdrücken Fähnien*)

Nickname: Devil's Nightmare, Double-Eagles, Drunken Alpine Truffles

Symbol: A stylized, black double-headed eagle on a gold field. The symbol is displayed on flags, banners, wagons, and tents.

Type: Standing/Fixed

Size: Legion; 418 (300)

Cost: 1620 gp/108 gp/800 per week (Contracts always include a clause for soldiers and camp followers to loot enemy dead on the battlefield)

Leader: *Hauptmann* Manferd Blöde (CN Human male Fighter 13)

Captains: 3; *Frau* Anjabeth Blöde (NG Human female Wizard 12), *Leutnant* Andreas Grauensteinen (LN Human male Fighter 12), *Freiherr* Gustav von Reischach (LN Human male Fighter 12)

Lieutenants: *FeldWeibel* Rölf Gruber, *Weibel* Hans Partenheimer, *Weibel* Danica Roon, *Weibel* Klaus Schumacher, *Weibel* Fritz Schumacher

Alignment: N

Formation: The company's primary unit is 300 *light foot* wielding 15' pikes. They are accompanied by 100 *heavy foot* who are armed with halberds (30), greatswords (30), and Calvoid made manarifles (40). Rounding out the company are 5 *mercenary acolytes*, 3 *mercenary priests*, and 10 *mercenary wizards*.

Expertise: Single/Sustained Battle

Trustworthiness: 4

Base: The Devil's Tower; Verigal (The Handle)

Sphere of Operations: Verigal (The Handle, Esta, Macehead), The Northern Savanna, The Desert of Urk, The Barren Islands

Government: Military Democracy

Tactics: Pikemen and halberdiers form a square in the center with greatsword wielding foot-soldiers to the front and rear. A wall of manariflemen surround the pikemen, who advance to fire, then drop back to reload and to allow the unit to march forward unimpeded.

The flexibility of the pike block cannot be understated, as it can change directions with two commands, and can even form a hedgehog (*Igel*) if beset from all sides. Pikes are held at chest height for combat with other infantry units, or the front three ranks of pikes can set their weapons braced against their feet in a lunge position, to ground them against a cavalry charge.

Camp followers, the spouses and sweethearts of the soldiers, also play a part in battle. They run water to the soldiers, and administer first aid if needed. After the battle, they loot the dead and dispatch wounded enemy soldiers who are not worth holding for ransom. They also help build battlements and set up the company's camp.

Logistics. Company soldiers are equipped with **above average** arms and some units have **superb** weapons and armor. Shortswords (*katzbalger*) are preferred to longswords, due to the close quarters of the pike block, but hand axes are used as well. The company does not use shields. The company keeps several armorers and smiths that keep weapons and armor in top shape. Officers frequently carry magical weapons and have numerous personal magical items. Foot soldiers are issued a *potion of healing* before major battles or sieges, and nearly 15% have a personal common or uncommon magical item. The non-combatants are almost always armed, mostly with daggers or shortswords and some (5%) will have a personal magical item. Soldiers and camp followers are allowed to keep any plunder found on the battlefield, as agreed to in the contract. All locked chest, however, are turned over to a company captain.

History. Like many on Shin'ar, most of the soldiers in the Devil's Regiment are not native to the planet. Three years ago, a portal opened and swallowed nearly two-hundred soldiers who were performing a siege of an enemy city. Just as the gates of the city were breached, and the invading army (including the Devil's Regiment) poured through the gap, the portal opened. Less than ten minutes later, it was closed, stranding the soldiers on Shin'ar. After the initial shock of the transfer wore off, the soldiers rallied around their commander, *Hauptmaan* Manferd Blöde, and worked to secure a fortified camp from which they could scout their new environs.

Within a day of their arrival, they came across villages and towns populated by humans, as well as beings whom the soldiers considered monstrous and alien. After communication was established, the Regiment was given probationary settling rights by the closest city-state, Medra. Weeks later, and after numerous meetings and discussions, the company's leader and captains petitioned the city-state of Medra for a formal mercenary company charter. Manferd understood that if his people were to thrive on this new planet, they must practice what they are good at, and they are good at making war.

Over the years, the company has integrated Vergal into their ranks, bringing their soldier compliment back to their pre-crossing numbers. After a successful campaign on the Barren Islands, the company was made honorary School members of the Spark's School of Law Keeping and Defense. In an unprecedented move, the Calvoid gifted the company a total of 40 manarifles, and the knowledge on how to manufacture hardened crystal bullets.

Prior to their crossing to Shin'ar, the *Landsknecht* mercenaries were known for their colored puff-and-slashed clothing, fierce demeanor, and fighting prowess. The company was founded 12 years ago when Manferd Blode was given a commission to raise troops to support an effort to reclaim contested lands. Manferd and Andreus Grauensteinen had served together as *Trabanten*, or bodyguards, to *Hauptmann* Otto von Bremerhaven in another mercenary company. When they were overrun during a battle, the other *Trabanten* fled, but Manferd and Andreus held fast and saved their commander, which allowed him to rally the troops and ultimately carry the day. As a reward for their bravery, they were given charge of a new unit. The two men rolled dice to see who would be the commander: Manferd lost.

The *Fähnlein* took it's name from an old proverb: the *Landsknecht* thrown out of Paradise can not enter into Hell, for he would make the Devil afraid. The soldiers spent the next eight years living up to that standard. They fought fiercely in major battles up and down the countryside, broke through besieging armies, captured enemy kings, and took part in the siege and razing of a major enemy city. It was during that last siege where the portal took most of the company to Shin'ar.

Hauptmann Manferd and his captains are always looking for news on how to return to their native world. A standing reward of 10,000 gold pieces has been offered to wizards and other learned individuals for any information on how to safely open a portal large enough to take them all through. But until then, they have resigned themselves to their fate, and live day-by-day doing what the love best in an alien land.

NEW WEAPON

Name	Cost	Damage	Weight	Properties
Manarifle	10,000 gp	1d12 piercing	13 lb.	Ammunition, range (60/120), mis-fire, mana dependent, penetration, loading

APPENDIX C CONVERSIONS

Many of the races, classes, and locations mentioned in the Tome of Mercenaries are pulled from two primary sources: The *Fifth Edition Player's Handbook*, and *Manastorm: World of Shin'ar*.

For those of you who do not own or have access to a copy of *Manastorm: World of Shin'ar*, you can easily convert any race or class to existing *PHB* races and classes by following the information listed. Conversions are not exact but match as close as possible while still maintaining some similar aspects and aesthetic.

MANASTORM: WORLD OF SHIN'AR (5E) RACES	5TH EDITION COMPATIBLE RACES
Aravork	Aarakocra
Calvoid	Gnome (Rock)
Drampyr	Drow
Frode	Halfling
Kalarin	Tabaxi
Rusk	Firbolg
Vampyr	Half-Elf (Drow)
Zevrish	Dwarf

MANASTORM: WORLD OF SHIN'AR (5E) CLASSES	5TH EDITION COMPATIBLE CLASSES
Aerialist	Ranger
Anointed Knight	Paladin
Geomancer	Monk/Sorcerer
Shadowgeist	Rogue
Spellknife	Rogue/Sorcerer
Technician	Wizard

MERCENARY CAPTAINS PLANING THE NEXT MISSION

84

Tome of Many Things

Terran Empire

DriveThruRPG
The *Largest* RPG Download Store

amazon

5th Edition Fantasy

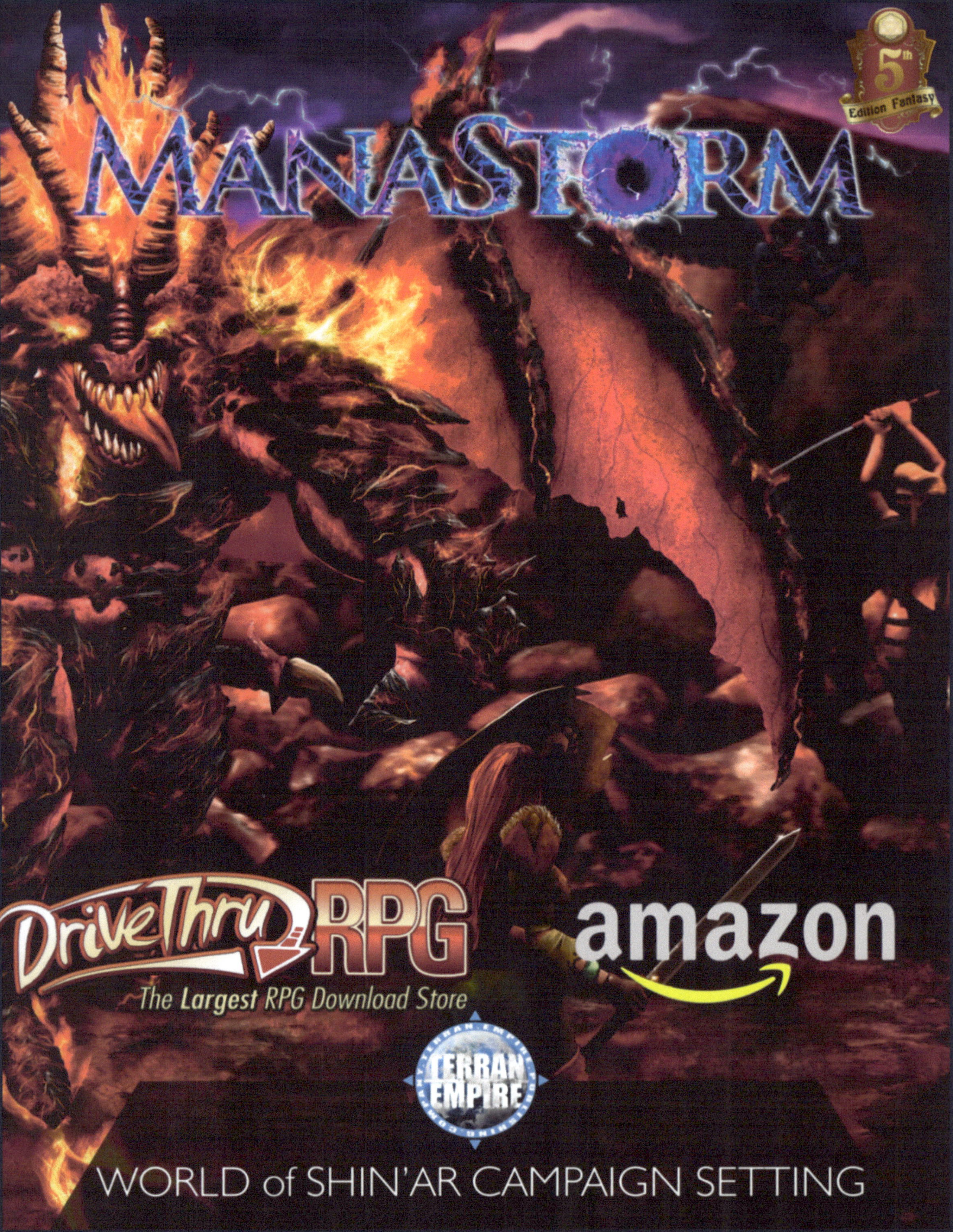
MANASTORM
5th Edition Fantasy
DriveThru RPG
The Largest RPG Download Store
amazon
TERRAN EMPIRE
WORLD of SHIN'AR CAMPAIGN SETTING

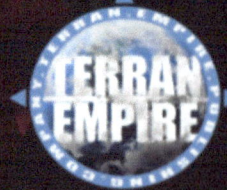